Herod Dreams

John Squires

Herod Dreams

John Squires

Published by
Mathom House Publishing
2008

Published by Mathom House Publishing
Mathom House
152 Carter Lane East
South Normanton
Derbyshire
DE55 2DZ

©John Squires 2008

A CIP catalogue record for this book
is available from the British Library

All rights are reserved. No parts of this book can be stored on a retrieval system or transmitted in any form or by whatever means without the prior permission in writing from the person holding the copyright.

Printed by Northend Creative Print Solutions, Sheffield

Cover design by Purple Circle Design Limited, Nottingham

ISBN 978-0-9559262-6-6

Herod Dreams

for

My family, past and present,

Ethan, the future,

The other clown, who believes.

From the Father:

Do not be afraid to read this. It will not harm you.

Remember, it is just a dream, and I am in a safe place.

You may become confused among the ghosts and angels on this journey and struggle to grasp its meaning.

Do not despair, dreams are like that.

Remember, this dream you hold in your hand.

You can return to it many times.

You may become lost and want to call out my name.

Remember, I am with you always and I will be there at the end, waiting for you.

Just because life is not everlasting does not mean it has no value or meaning. Life is so sweet.

Remember, it does not come again, so find time to taste it.

Now it begins...

In the beginning…

"Hear my prayer.
All flesh shall come before
you."

Introit and Kyrie

He called himself Herod.

An old woman found the first child's body in a small glade of trees while walking her dog. The body had been sealed in a black plastic bag.

Soon, two more were found in different parts of the country. Both in plastic bags.

He walked into our station one wet afternoon and asked for me. I did not recognise him, of course, but he knew me.
'I know you,' he said.
He told me his name but I still could not remember.
He said that he had done enough and that he wanted to stop. He had come to confess to it all.
We sat in the interview room and he described in detail what he had done. How he had not chosen the children but had left that to chance or fate or God.
I knew he spoke the truth because he knew details that had not been released to the media. He knew about the eyes he had taken and the notes he had left.
When I asked about why he had done it, he smiled and could see that I still did not recognise him. He sat back in his chair.
'You still don't remember me, do you?'
I shook my head.
'We have met before. A long time ago. I asked for your help then, when my faith was tested. And you helped me.'

I shook my head again.

'It was a long time ago,' he said. 'It will come to you in time.'

And he smiled again, as though he knew me for what I was.

We took him to the holding cell, where he was stripped of anything he could use to harm himself. As I closed the cell door, I heard him call out.

It was then I remembered the journey and the nightmares began…

"Thy faith
hath made thee whole."

The dream of the mother…

"Deliver the souls of the
dead from the pain of hell."

Offertory

1

The journey had not begun well. She had woken with a headache, having slept badly again. The airport lounge, filled with lost souls made her nervous, and a cup of coffee had only made her feel sick. And now, as they were boarding, there was a problem. The seats that they had pre-booked months ago were needed. Could they move? And, of course, he agreed. They had not asked her, not recognised her as a decision maker. How could they? She was not wearing her suit. And, in some ways, she was grateful. The whole of this holiday was to be an escape from decision- making and responsibility.

And then they found their new seats. They had pre-booked so that she could sit by a window, gaze down at the world passing by and look out for the lone ships in the vast ocean below. Now she found herself in an aisle seat next to the toilets and her head pounded and the vomit lay in her stomach, waiting.

Her husband settled himself into the tight space and began to make small talk to the man next to her window. She closed her eyes and listened to the sound of the aircraft preparing to leave. Two hours and they would be in Portugal. Two more hours and they would be at the villa, away from all this.

They had found the Casa Ra many years ago when their son was young. It was on a small lemon farm, a few miles from a village called Guia. That holiday had been memorable for visits to crowded towns and beaches and days out to water parks, which she had hated. What she had loved had been the villa's seclusion, being able to swim unafraid in the pool and to return from a restaurant at night to sit and gaze at the stars. And that was what this holiday was going to be; pool, restaurants and stars. The hours in between would be filled with light reading and carefree visits to quiet places.

She was woken as the plane landed at Faro. The sweet aroma of the toilets clung to her. After the cramped bus ride to the terminal and the passport check, she took two more pills while he dragged their cases from the luggage belt. Despite directions to the car hire, they got lost and, by the time they reached the place, the queue was already outside the building in blazing midday heat. She found some shade and sat with the cases, while he waited in line.

The car was a small Fiesta. It was all they needed. He heaved their suitcases into the back of the car. She sorted through the bag and found the directions to the villa. This was her only responsibility for today. Every holiday he would drive and she would do her best to navigate. The driving was not something he had taken from her. He was not like that. It was just that she hated driving and dreaded the thought of having to drive on the wrong side of the road. He sat beside her and began to sort out the controls. Already she was gripped by the fear that something would go wrong. It had last time. Last time they had missed the motorway and ended up in Loule, without maps, and that had been her responsibility. She read through the directions again and looked out at the crowded car park.

'Okay,' he sighed. 'How do we get out of here?'

She saw it before him, a great, brown dog loping along the side of the main road.
'Look out!'
'What?'
There was a slight thud as they passed.
'Oh, no!'
'What? What's the matter?'
She pulled away her seat belt and turned to look back.
'What are you doing?'
She peered through the back window, hoping that the dog would be all right. All she could see was the car behind them. The passenger in the car seemed to be also turning to look back.
'You hit a dog…'
'What?'
'You hit a dog!'
'I didn't see any dog…'
He looked into the mirror.
'Are you sure?'
'You've got to stop.'
'I can't stop here…Look! There's the turning for the motorway.'
He indicated and followed the slip road's tight curve onto the motorway. Her heart was pounding. Cars and lorries roared passed them.
'I didn't see it, love! It'll probably be all right…I couldn't have hit it hard…I didn't feel anything.'
The motorway snaked ahead through the burnt ground.

Finding the exit was easy and as they drove along the N125 they began to talk to each other again.

'My God,' he sighed. 'This is getting just like America. They even have shopping malls now!'

They passed between the Algarve Shopping centre and a large Makro outlet.

'According to the directions the turning to go through Guia should be soon.

'Be careful, it's one of those funny left turns, like in Spain. You have to go right to turn left.'

'Look at this place. I don't remember it being like this. Do you?'

'It has been nearly ten years, love. There's bound to have been some changes.'

They negotiated the turn and began to recognise the village.

'There's the road with the restaurants,' he laughed. 'And the pharmacy. And the telephone box…I know where I am now…God! Look! They even have apartment blocks here now!'

'At least they're only two storeys high.'

'I know…but in Guia!'

She knew it was not far now and began to relax, loosening her grip on the door handle and beginning to forget the dog. After a few kilometres they came to a turn in the road protected by a crash barrier.

'It should be here,' she warned. 'Just on the right. Don't miss it. It's easy to miss.'

She could feel herself becoming agitated; concerned that he would drive past the turning and have to brake hard. He always drove too fast. But ahead of them were traffic lights that changed to red so he had to stop.

'We're here,' she said. 'Look, just there. That's the white house where we turn.'

The lights changed and he turned out of the road onto a dusty, stone track.

'This is it!' he cheered. 'That's the house where they had all those puppies outside! Remember, love? And he wanted to bring one home with him. We're here!'

The tyres crunched over the track, spitting out jagged stones and crushing baked earth. And she smiled at his child-like enthusiasm as they wound their way back to Casa Ra.

It looked the same. They got out of the car into the bright, reflected sunlight. She climbed the three steps to the terrace with its small shaded area by the wall and saw the pool. It was the same. While she gazed across the pool, across the tops of the small lemon trees in the valley of the lemon farm, across to the far hill, he dragged the suitcases out of the car and came to join her.

'Isn't it lovely?'

'Yes,' he smiled. 'Come on; let's see how we get in.'

He punched in the code to get the door key and handed it to her.

'It won't open.'

She could feel the panic beginning to rise again.

'It must do.'

She turned the handle again and pushed.

'No. It won't.'

'It could be a double lock. Turn the key again, love.'

She turned the key and could feel it release the second lock but when she turned the handle again nothing happened. He could see the panic in her face and tried

13

the handle. The door would not open.

'What are we going to do?'

'It's okay. There must be a trick in it somehow.'

He re-locked the door and tried again. She could hear the lock releasing. Once. Twice. And then the door opened!

'It just opens with the key. Quick. What's the code for the alarm?'

She handed him the piece of paper.

'It should be on the left, by the fridge.'

'Found it.'

He pressed the buttons on the keypad and breathed a deep sigh of relief.

'Done it.'

Suddenly the siren's piercing scream filled the air. She covered her ears and watched as he frantically punched in the code again. The sound tore at her, trying to force her out of the house.

'Do something! Please!' she shouted but could hardly hear herself.

She could see that he was trying to make sense of the instructions on the alarm's cover. He pressed the buttons again and the alarm suddenly fell silent. The effort seemed to have exhausted him.

'It hadn't been switched on.'

'But the instructions said…'

'I know, love…But it wasn't…I'll bring the cases in.'

She felt the weariness in his voice and said, 'Just leave them for a moment. Let's go up to the balcony and have a look out over the fields.'

'No, I need to bring them in. You go up. I'll bring them up. The same bedroom I suppose?'

She smiled.

'Let's hope the bed's softer than last time!'
The sound of her sandals echoed through the house, as she climbed the tiled stairs. She turned on the light to see through the gloom of the shuttered bedroom and noticed that the bed had not been made. Suddenly there were people talking downstairs. She thought of the dog and hoped it wasn't the police.
'You early…No clean!'
It was the maid.
'Sorry…Alarm not on…Make loud noise,' he tried to explain.
'You early…Me clean.'
'Of course…Sorry…We thought one o'clock okay.'
'Early…Me clean!'
'Yes…Sorry…We go.'
He turned and smiled at her as she came down the stairs.
'My wife here…We go…Can we leave the cases here…Cases…Leave…Here?'
'Yes…Sorry…Must clean…Sorry.'
She gathered her mop and bucket and went to the sink.
'How long will you be?' he asked, pointing to his watch. 'Time…When finish clean?
They could see she was searching for the words.
'One hour?' he suggested.
'Yes…Good…One hour…Clean.'
She pulled the bucket from the sink and carried it up the stairs.
They went outside and sat beneath the small canopy that offered the only shade.
'What do you want to do then?'
'I don't know.'
'Why don't we go back to the Algarve Shopping? At

least it's got air conditioning there, I presume. And we could look for some supplies.'

'Yes…It's supposed to have a hypermarket. We need to get fruit and some cheese and drinks,' she agreed, glad that they would at least be doing something.

'We'd have to have done it later anyway,' he continued, seeing her mood lighten.

'Yes, you're right.'

'Let's just check the car.'

He saw the change in her expression.

'If I hit it, there might be a mark. I don't think there will be but just to…'

She led the way to the car and they checked the bodywork.

'What's this?'

She pointed to a patch of deep scratches by the wheel arch.

'That was there when I got the car, love.'

'Are you sure?'

'Yes…Someone must have backed into a concrete post or a rock or something. They marked it down on a form at the rental place…Really.'

He got into the car and she guided him out of the driveway. As she fastened her seat belt, he assured her that he could find his way back to the shopping mall. Everything was fine, now. He knew where he was and what to do. All she needed to do was to sit. They could think about what to buy when they got there. There was no pressure. He drove carefully back along the track, stopped between a wall and the end of a white farm house to check it was safe to continue and it was there that she saw them. Two dogs tied to a tree. As he manoeuvred past them, they scramble to their feet and began to bark. Great, savage, gaping mouths that filled her with fear. They tried to chase after the car but crashed to the ground, held back by the ropes that tied them to the tree.

Reaching the Algarve shopping centre was easier than she had anticipated and, when they had parked the car, he suggested that, as they had plenty of time, they should explore, see if there were any shops where they might buy gifts for their friends later on.
There were the usual outlets that could be found anywhere in the world, but at least they offered welcome relief from the heat that blanketed the uncovered walkways. Eventually they found a food outlet area and she sent him to get some croissants and coffees, while she found a clean table. She brushed the crumbs off the plastic chair, sat down and began to watch the people passing by. Many were families, trying to decide where to eat and she recognised the frustration on the mothers' faces as they were left to organise everything.
He joined her, carrying a bright yellow tray.
'I got a plain croissant for you and a chocolate one for me.'
'What's that?'
'I thought I'd try an espresso.'
'That's adventurous!'
'Well, we're on holiday, love.'
She laughed and took her things from the tray.
'You be careful,' she said. 'It could go right to your head.'
'I'll be all right.'
He picked up the cup and took a sip.

'God, that's hot!'
'What do you expect? You've no milk with it.'
'I'll just eat this then. Let it cool down.'
He took a bite from the croissant and chocolate oozed out from the sides. A child began to scream.
'Somebody's upset,' he chuckled, turning in his seat.
'Don't stare at them! It's just some child not getting its own way.'
'Thank God we've left that behind.'
'He was never like that! I can't remember him ever screaming if he didn't get what he wanted.'
'No, he never did, did he. He was always well behaved.'
'He still is.'
'Yes, love. We were very lucky. I hope he and his wife are as lucky with their child, when they have one.'
'I thought we weren't going to talk about that!'
'Of course…Sorry…Did you see anything in the shops?'
'No, not yet.'

He took another bite of the croissant and felt the side of his cup. It was still too hot to drink. He knew he had upset her by talking about the possibility of having a grandchild. Her son had been happily married for a few years and yet there was still no sign. He looked around for something else to talk about and noticed an old lady cleaning tables. She cleared the debris into a black bag and wiped over the table-tops with a wet cloth. He watched her as she moved methodically from table to table. Eventually she reached a table where a small child was sitting alone, strapped to her invalid chair. The old lady cleared the plates and wrappings from the table and seemed to be speaking to the girl.

He looked around, but could see no parents. And then something strange happened. The old lady removed the straps from the chair, took a black plastic bag from her trolley, wrapped it around the girl so that it covered her completely and, with amazing ease, raised the girl from her chair. The girl did not struggle, did not call out. And no one seemed to notice! Everyone around them continued to eat and to talk as though nothing was happening. He called out, but no one heard him. He turned to his wife.
'Look at that!'
'What?'
'Over there!'
He turned back to point and saw that they had gone.
'What's the matter?'
'I just saw…'
'What?'
He looked around. There was nothing. Just people.
'Are you alright?'
He could see the concern on her face.
'Yes, love. I must have been seeing things.'
'What was it?'
'Nothing…nothing.'
'I told you that coffee would be strong.'
He laughed and picked up the cup. The coffee was still too hot. He could feel his heart racing and searched for something to say, something that would break the confusion between them.
'I bet they're British, look.'
He nodded towards a family entering the area.
'How can you tell that?' she scoffed.
'Well, they're as pale as us and the fact that man's wearing a knotted handkerchief on his head is a bit of a

giveaway, don't you think?'

She laughed and he smiled.

And they drank their coffee. And they ate their croissants. And, together, they watched the people pass by.

It was much cooler inside the hypermarket. Within its vastness they found the fresh fruit, cheese, juices, milk and healthy cereals for the meals they would have at the villa; food that would help to cleanse her. But, of course, he had to have his treats; cakes, biscuits and bottles of his favourite fizzy drink and so he spent ages dithering by the shelves, trying to make up his mind what to choose. And he was right to take his time. There was no pressure. It was not like the tedious Saturday's supermarket ordeal, when she would fight her way through the masses, chained to the dreaded list and weighed down by the lack of time. Grapes looked like grapes and Brie looked like Brie, no matter what the labels on the shelves said. She could browse. If they forgot something, then it didn't matter. They could return tomorrow.

On the way back to the car, he seemed to stagger for an instant. She caught hold of his arm.

'What's the matter?'

'Nothing…I just felt dizzy for a moment. It must be that coffee.'

'Do you want me to carry something?'

'No, love. I'm all right.'

They found the car, loaded the shopping and drove back to the villa.

The two dogs ignored them.

'Perhaps it was the heat,' she thought.

After they had unpacked he persuaded her to play a game of pool in a shaded area by the side of the villa.
She had not really wanted to. He knew that she hated that sort of thing. They had never played any of his games together. She had tried to learn to play chess and his beloved golf but had quickly become frustrated by her lack of competence and given up. Now he never played chess and hardly ever ventured onto a golf course. He showed her how to hold a cue, let her practise a few shots and then they began a game. She knew that he was setting up the shots so that she would be able to knock in a few balls and that he was deliberately missing his own. It came as no surprise to her that she won the game. He set up for the next game and won that quite comfortably. By then she had had enough and they went to get a cool drink. She collected her book and found some shade. He surprised her by appearing in his trunks.
'What are you doing?'
'I thought I'd have a dip in the pool…A few lengths…to cool down. Are you coming in?'
'Not now, I've just got my book.'
'Later?'
She could hear the farm labourers in the fields below and knew they would be finishing for the day. That meant they would be parking their lorry at the end of the track soon. Standing on the back of the lorry they could see over the wall. She was not ready for that.
'No…I'll stay in the shade for now. You know how my skin burns…perhaps tomorrow.'
She watched him as he gingerly entered the water.
'You big baby!' she teased.

'I can feel them shrinking back into my body,' he joked.
He took the last step into the shallow end of the pool and began to splash the water over his shoulders.
'Brrrr,' he shuddered. 'It's not so bad when you're in.'
He began to breaststroke to the deep end.
'In fact, it's lovely,' he called
'Tomorrow,' she thought. 'Tomorrow.'

That evening they went into Guia and tried to find the restaurant they had visited before. It had been their favourite restaurant. Good food. Good atmosphere. They had been there many times because they had enjoyed it so much and the waiters had always fussed over them, especially their young son with his long blonde hair. To their surprise, it had moved across the street. It was smaller now. The fish they ordered seemed dry and the vegetables were over cooked. By eight o'clock, it was filled with English tourists. By nine o'clock, they had had enough. They paid the bill and left.
'Let's walk,' she said, as they stepped out into the darkness. 'We don't have to go back yet.'
'Fine,' he said. 'Perhaps we could find another restaurant.'
They left the car and strolled along the main road passing the football bar, the small market and the school.
'If we turn left here,' he said. 'We head back into the village.'
She could see it was barely a road and there was no footpath. She held his hand.
'Okay.'

The first restaurant was surrounded by badly parked cars. Nothing on the dimly lit menu appealed to them. This section of road had no lighting and they had to rely on the headlights of the cars as they passed. Eventually they could see the streetlights again. It was part of Guia they had not been to before. On the right hand side she noticed a subdued light on a balcony. People were talking and drinking. They crossed over and squeezed past some large limousines. Although it looked like a large house and no sound came from the ground floor, there was a menu outside for the Casa. They read through it.
'This looks different,' she said.
'It's a bit expensive.'
'Not that much more. And the menu is good.'
He could feel the excitement in her.
'Shall we try it tomorrow, then?'
'Yes,' she said. 'I'd like that.'
She snuggled into his arm and he felt the warmth of her happiness.
'Come on then. Let's find the car. I think I can smell the sewers now!'
'Oh, you!'
She gave him a playful punch on the arm and he smiled. They crossed between the cars, found the narrow pavement and made their way down to the village. Behind them the Casa sat in its darkness, waiting for their return.

That night she did not sleep well. It was not the bed, nor the fans in the room. She lay awake, listening to his snoring as usual. She didn't mind that so much. She knew she could wake him and make him turn over. He would do the same to her. They often teased each other about who had snored the most in the night. No, it was the dog barking in the distance. And for some reason the sound filled her with fear.

She woke late in the morning and could not tell if it was still night. The shutters blocked out any sunlight.
'Are you awake?'
He grunted.
'Shall I make a cup of tea?'
'What time is it?'
'I don't know. Are you all right?'
'Yes, love.'
'No headache?'
Usually the stress of travelling and driving gave him a headache on the first day.
'No. I'm okay; I think…Shall I put the light on?'
'Yes, please.'
She found her glasses and looked at her watch.
'It's half past ten!'
'Good!'
She got out of bed and went down to make the tea. When she opened the shutters in the kitchen, the light blinded her. Water for the kettle. Teabags. Milk from the fridge. She switched the fans on to move the air and heard him coming down the stairs.
'What's the matter?'
'I might need some pills after all.'
'Oh, no, love…they're in the canvas bag. Do you want me to get them?'
'No. I'll find them.'
He searched through the bag, while she poured the boiling water into the mugs.

'Haven't found a teapot, yet,' she grumbled and carried a sopping teabag to the bin.
'Oh, no!'
'What?'
'Look!'
The thick, black bin liner was covered in ants.
'It must be the bits of fruit I left in there yesterday.'
He carefully peeled the liner away from the bin and shook the ants into the bottom of the bag. He sealed it and tried to lift it out. The dead weight seemed to cling to the bin.
'Are you sure it was just fruit?' he asked, struggling to force the black bag out. The bin clattered on to hard tiles, as the black mass fell against his legs. He could feel the inside bag moving against his feet, as though something was trying to get out.
'What else could it be?'
'Well, look at it.'
'It could be the ants at the bottom…'
'There must be thousands!' he gasped.
'Well, take them out! We can't have them in the house!'
'We'll have to get some powder or something.'
'Take them out!'
He opened the door and the sunlight burst into the room.
'God! It's hot out here!'

The tea did not taste right. There was something wrong with the water. A ring of brown slime slid down the inside of the mugs.
'We can forget about that, then,' he grumbled.
'I did try!'
'It's not your fault, love. It's just the water.'

He tried another mouthful.
'No…can't drink that.'
Putting the mug on the bedside table, he turned to her.
'Well, what shall we do today?'
'Are you going to be all right?'
'Yes…I'll be okay…It's not that bad and now I've taken the pills…I tell you what, let's go to the hypermarket, get something for the ants, have a look round and have a cup of coffee again. By the time we get back the maid will have been and we can have the rest of the day by the pool.'
'Okay.'
'Erm…there's just one thing though,' he warned.
'What's that?'
'It's your turn to shower first!'
'Oh, no!'
'Oh, yes! You know the rule. First one up always showers first!'
'But I'm on holiday!'
'Go on!'
She grabbed her pillow and threw it at him.
'Violence isn't going to get you anywhere, young lady,' he laughed.
She kicked off the sheet and got out of bed.
'You're a big bully, you are!' she teased and went down the stairs.
He lay back in bed and smiled.
The shower cubicle shared a space with a toilet and washbasin. She put the clean, white towel over the washbasin and took off her nightdress. She caught sight of herself in the mirror and knew that she was not a young lady, no matter how many times he said it. Childbirth and time had taken their toll. No matter

how many times she had tried, she could not get rid of the weight. Dieting became a chore inflicted on the rest of the family, as they felt her resentment during meals. Exercise was a bore and was not even considered, despite the constant badgering to join a gym. The thought of exposing her body in public filled her with shame. Only he would see her. She turned on the shower and it ran cold for a long time. She was beginning to think she had done something wrong and would have to call him again, when she felt the first warmth on her hand. Gradually the water got too hot and she had to turn the dial a few times before she could get in to the cubicle. The warm water streamed over her. She crossed her arms under her breasts and let the water gather in small pools. Eventually she took the soap from the dish and washed her body in the smallest cubicle in the Algarve.

It was nearly mid-day when they left. They drove between the wall and the farmhouse, expecting to be attacked by the two dogs again. But, as they passed, the dogs did not even stir from their narrow patch of shade. It was as if they did not exist.
'What's wrong with them?' she asked, turning back to see if they had moved.
'Probably too hot to even care.'
He pulled onto the main road and they headed to the hypermarket.
They spent an hour drinking their coffees; eating their croissants and watching people go by. She found herself making snap judgements about individuals, couples and families, summing up their lives with no real justification at all. The chair was feeling

uncomfortable and the table was too hard to lean against.
'Can we go now?'
'See those two over there,' he murmured, nodding towards two young men. 'Queers.'
'Stop that!'
'They are! I've been watching them.'
She knew he had said it to get some reaction from her, but the joke had not worked. It had only made her feel worse about her own preconceptions.
'What's the matter?'
She gathered up the canvas bag.
'Let's go and get the things we need.'
'It was only a joke!'
'I know.'

They found some ant spray with a little help and browsed through the aisles until they came to the drinks section.
'I know, love,' he said with some excitement. 'Let's get some Cointreau and ice. We could have it tonight on the balcony, beneath the stars.'
Of course! She had forgotten. Last night, because they were so exhausted, they had just fallen into bed. Of course! The stars!
'That's a great idea,' she smiled.
He put the bottle of Cointreau into the basket and they searched for some ice.

When they got back to the villa, it smelt fresh and clean.
'The maid must have been,' she announced, as he punched in the code for the alarm. They both held

their breath, waiting for the high-pitched scream to explode into the room. But the system blip-blipped and settled into its ordered silence.

'Thank God for that,' he sighed. She unpacked the plastic bag and put the ice into the freezer, while he studied the can of ant spray.

'It's all in Portuguese.'

'What do you expect?'

'It can't be any different from ours.'

He shook the can and began to search for the ants in the cupboard under the sink. He soon found the trail and followed it along the kitchen floor tight against the sides of the cabinets.

'Here it is!'

There was a small hole between the wall and the tile. He sprayed along the trail and into the cupboard.

'That should do it…Do you want me to get the ones outside?'

'No. I just don't want them in the house…Do you want a cold drink? I thought we could have it outside and read for a while, before we have lunch.'

'That sounds fine to me. We need to get out from this smell anyway, I should think.'

The odour from the spray was beginning to irritate the back of their noses and their throats, like a soft burning.

'I need to go up to get changed and put some more cream on,' she said. 'You go out and I'll bring you a drink when I come down.'

He collected his book and glasses from the table and listened to the clap-clap of her sandals on the tiled stairway.

The covered area on the terrace offered no shade from the afternoon sun and he took his book down to sun loungers by the edge of the pool. He adjusted the back of the lounger so that he could sit and read and then set about re-arranging the sun umbrellas to make some shade. He had just sat down and opened his book when she appeared. The ice clinked in the glasses as she came down the steps and around the edge of the pool.

'This is nice,' she smiled and handed him his soft drink. The outside of the glass was cold and wet. He put it on the dry, baked tile floor and moved slightly so that she could pass.

'You look lovely.'

She was wearing a large, light cotton dress, covered in African prints. As she moved it flowed about her body.

'It covers me up.'

'Have you put plenty of cream on?'

'Yes.'

She passed through his shade and settled into the shade he had made for her.

'What are you reading?'

'Oh, just some usual airport trash,' she laughed. 'Holiday reading. Nothing too arduous. You know me!'

She was uncomfortable, turned and re-adjusted the back of her lounger.

'Sorry,' he said. 'I thought it would be all right like it was.'

She clicked the back of the lounger into its new position.

'It's okay. What have you got?'

'Some Chekhov short stories.'
'God!'
'Raymond Carver talked about him in his book of poetry I read. I thought I'd give him a try.'
'I saw one of his plays a long time ago. The Three Sisters or something like that. I didn't see the point of it all.'
'I thought I'd give him a try.'
She settled back into the chair.
'They weren't too friendly when we drove back.'
'Who?'
'The people at the farmhouse down the track…Near the dogs. I waved to the old woman but she ignored me.'
'Perhaps she didn't see you.'
'In the car?'
'No. I mean waving…She didn't see you waving.'
'She must have done. She was looking straight at us…It was like we weren't there. She looked straight through me.'
He leaned over to pick up his drink. A thin trail of ants had already discovered the ring of cool water at the bottom of the glass.
After half an hour he had had enough. It was too hot and the ants had begun to annoy him. They were finding their way onto his legs and beginning to bite.
'Right, that's it!' he announced, flicking another ant away. 'I've had enough. I'm going to have a swim. The water should be just right by now. Do you fancy a dip?'
She peered at him over her glasses.
'I'll just finish this chapter.'
'Watch out for the ants. Now I've gone, they'll

probably come looking for you.'

The line of ants stretched from the edge of the pool, under their loungers, across the tiled area and down through a drainage pipe into a garden area below them. He carried the glass and his book into the house and went up to the bedroom to change.

Absorbed in her book, she was not aware of his presence until she heard him gasping and complaining as he entered the water. She peered over her glasses.

'Don't start!' he warned, jokingly.

'I didn't say a word.'

'You didn't have to. I know you! Just give me time. Let me do it in my own way.'

She watched, as he timidly lowered himself into pool, like a young child. He had always been thin. Skinny. Barely nine stone wet through, as his mother used to say. But now, middle-aged spread and lack of exercise had piled on the weight and his body sagged in its old skin. He splashed the water over his shoulders and launched himself into his favourite breaststroke. As he reached the far end of the pool he turned and beamed at her.

'There you are!' he called across the shimmer. 'Are you coming?'

She felt the ants beginning to bite at her ankle and brushed them away. She could see more of them starting to search for her. She marked her place in the book.

'You just wait there for me,' she smiled and picked up the glass.

'It's lovely when you get used to it,' he called and set off on his second length.

In the bedroom she found her costume and put it on.

It had been a whole year since she had last worn it and she felt awkward, as she inspected herself in the mirror. She knew the farmers would not be back for at least two hours so no one should see. She closed her eyes to ignore what was in the mirror and took a deep breath.

'You only want me for my body,' she had said, when they were lovers and newly married and they had laughed in their deep passion for each other. She picked up the African dress and a towel and headed down to the pool in her bare feet.

She could see that he had been swimming for some time and his hair was wet from being under the water. She placed the towel and dress over a rail and, without hesitating, walked down the steps into the pool.

'How do you do that?' he called out in astonishment. 'How can you just glide into the water like that?'

'Like what?'

'Like some goddess!'

'Don't be silly!'

They swam towards each other.

'It's good this, isn't it?' he laughed.

'Wonderful!' she agreed and swam slowly away to the end of the pool.

She let the water carry her and its coolness caressed her body. Floating in its gentleness, she began to feel herself relax. She swam slowly and without effort, resting in the shade that covered the shallow end of the pool when she needed to.

Sometimes they would meet and he would hold her and she would know that he still desired her body.

'That's nice,' she said as she leant back against him and felt his hands against her breast as he held her in the water. They stood like that for while and then he, unsure of himself and the situation, broke free and swam away.

'I'm going to do six lengths and then get changed,' he called back to her.

She watched him complete his mini-marathon and get out of the pool. The water drained from his trunks and splashed onto the dry tiles. He rubbed the towel into his hair and dried his shoulders.

'I'm just going to have a little longer,' she said and ploughed her way to the deep end.

He stood in the heat of the sun, his wet trunks clinging to him. When she turned, she caught sight of him and gasped. He was standing with his back to her, naked, about to go into the house.

When she got out of the pool and went inside, he was already showering. She closed the door behind her, took off her costume, wrapped herself in the towel, climbed the stairs and waited on the bed. She heard him come out of the shower room and hoped he might call up to her but the sudden blare of the television told her that he would not be coming. She took her dressing gown from the back of a chair and went down.

'Have you finished in the shower?' she asked, with no hint of disappointment.

'Yes, love.'

'Only you didn't call…'

'Sorry…I thought I'd catch up on the news from home. You can get the BBC.'

'Are you getting dressed up?'

'I thought I'd just have light trousers and a shirt. It looked a bit posh for shorts and…'

'Yes. That should be all right.'
She pushed the shower room door closed behind her.
The mirror was covered in condensation. She let the water run for a while and then washed the chlorine from her body.

They left the car in the small car park behind the market and crossed the main road to the telephone box outside the football club bar. She tried three times to contact her son, to let him know they were safe, but each time all she could hear was the engaged tone.
'That's strange,' she said.
'Well, you know what he's like.'
'But I told him we would phone today at this time,' she grumbled.
'We'll try later.'
'He'll be out at work.'
'Tomorrow, then.'
The traffic was tailing back from the main crossroad and the side streets were filling with cars trying to find a place to park.
'I hope we didn't need to book.'
He knew it was a complaint thrown in his direction.
'We'll be all right, I should think.'
'Perhaps we should have booked last night.'
'Let's see shall we…I would have thought they would have a table for two. It's only five past seven.'
At first she thought they might have taken a wrong turn, but then she saw it. In the melee of drivers trying to park their cars in the narrow street, the Casa seemed to be waiting for them in its own pool of silence at the fork in the road. Beside the entrance, leaning against the wall, were three large black plastic bags, sealed tight.

When they entered through the gateway, they were confused. The ground floor room seemed to be deserted. There was no sign of life. A second door led straight back out on to the street. Slightly embarrassed, he called out but no one answered. A blood-red, concrete staircase was the only other way out of the room.

'It must be up here,' he decided and began to climb.

Even though there was no handrail to hold and the stairs were quite steep, she had a strange sensation that she was almost floating up the stairway as she followed him. At the top, on a small landing, was a wine rack. To their left they could see part of a room containing a sink, cupboards and a desk. To their right was a curtain. He hesitated for a moment and then pulled back the curtain. The room was so warm and welcoming in its simple beauty that they both gasped in surprise and delight.

'This is lovely!'

She felt the curtain drift across her back as it closed behind them and, to her amazement, she began to hear a favourite piece of classical music playing quietly in the background. Still, no one had come to meet them.

'There must be somebody around,' he said.

'Who's that?'

To their left, outside on the terrace, they could make out the figure of what looked like a man sitting on a chair. His back was turned to them. They held hands and walked together to the doorway. The man seemed unaware of their presence. He sat, gazing into the distance, and she felt it would be wrong to disturb his meditation, but what else was there to do?

'Good evening,' she said and was shocked to realise that she had broken the silence.

The man turned to them and rose from the chair. 'Ah, Madame,' he smiled. 'Forgive me. I was daydreaming…Welcome…Please take a seat.'

A bench set into the wall of the terrace formed the seating area with small, round tables for drinks.

'What can I get you to drink, Madame?'

'Could I have a dry white wine, please? A Sauvignon Blanc?'

'Certainly, Madame…Sir?'

'Just a soft drink for me, please…I'm driving.'

'I think I have just the thing, sir. Here are the menus for you.'

He handed the menus to them and left to fetch the drinks. From the terrace they could look across what appeared to be deserted land to the car park they had used. Immediately behind them were the ruins of a row of small houses. To their right, at the top of the hill, new apartments were being built.

'What are you going to have?' he asked.

'I don't know yet,' she replied. 'There are some interesting starters. I like the sound of the prawns in chilli and honey sauce.'

'I was looking at that as well.'

'Don't tell me we're going to have the same things again,' she laughed. They now seemed to order the same things whenever they went out for a meal. It was as though their tastes in food were becoming identical. The man returned.

'Forgive me,' he said, handing them their drinks. 'I have forgotten the blind.'

Across the far side of the terrace was a large blind. As

he raised it, they saw the tops of the village houses below them and, in the distance, the sun above the hills of Monchique. 'That's really beautiful,' she said.

'If the sun becomes too bright you must tell me,' he smiled.

'Is that what made you buy this place?' her husband asked. 'The view?'

'No, sir' the owner replied politely. 'This house belonged to an old, local family. It was built on a special piece of ground. A safe place between two roads.'

'How long have you been here, then?' he continued.

The owner smiled.

'Oh, a long time, sir.'

'There have been a lot of changes since we were last here. Lots of new apartments have gone up.'

'Yes, sir.'

'It used to be just a little village.'

'Yes, but it has always been known as a place to eat. There are lots of restaurants and Guia is close to the beaches and the motorway. It is becoming quite the place to live.'

'We couldn't help but notice the derelict houses and the wasteland.'

'Yes, sir. All this you see across to the car park. The owners are waiting for the right price to sell. The price is high now but they think it may go higher and so they are waiting in the hope they might make a fortune.'

'And the houses?'

'The same reason, sir. They are neglected because their owners hope to become rich in the future.'

The waitress appeared with a tray on which was their couvert. They were used to this by now. It happened in all the restaurants. A tray of appetisers, while the order was taken and the starters prepared. It was usually a small tin of sardine pate, dry bread, a portion of butter and a small dish of black olives, which she hated. But this was completely different.

'I'll leave you to choose your meals.'

The owner and waitress disappeared into the restaurant. She watched them looking out of the restaurant windows into the street below and she heard the people passing by. No one was coming up the stairs to join them. They were on the terrace, alone.

She felt the chill of the wine through her glass and caught the fresh, fruit bouquet as she brought it to her lips. The taste was perfect. As she browsed through the menu, she took some bread from the tray. It was warm, soft and melted in her mouth. There were small bites to eat, which tasted delicious. Why had they not found this place before? She caught sight of her husband studying his menu and smiled. Behind him, over the hills of Monchique, the sky was beginning to turn red.

When the waitress returned, they ordered the same things.

'It looks as though it is going to be a quiet night,' the owner smiled as he joined them.

'You were busy last night when we came past.'

'Yes, sir. It was a changeover day for our visitors. They usually come here on their first day or their last. A sort of celebration for them...But tonight, we are very quiet.'

'Does that make it difficult for business?'

'Oh, I have given up planning for each day a long time

ago. You can never tell, sir. Some days we have to turn people away.'
'We hear you are having a problem with fires.'
'Because of the drought, sir. Yes, in the North there have been many fires. It is strange, this weather. Here we have serious droughts but, in other places in Europe, there are severe floods.'
'Really?'
'Yes, sir. Many people are drowned and their houses destroyed by the floods.'
'Have there been fires here?'
'Not this year. But, some years ago, there were fires in the Monchique mountains. Oh, yes, Madame. You could see the smoke from here. When it had finished, my wife and I drove up there and everywhere was burnt. Just terrible. But you know, Madame, a few months later, in the spring, we drove up again and we saw the green shoots on the ground and on the trees. It was wonderful to see how nature could recover so quickly. Even when you would have thought that all was lost.'
'Do you live here?'
'I live in Silves, sir. You have been there?'
'When we came with the children, we drove through there. It's where the Moors had their fort?'
'That is correct, sir. Did you visit the fort?'
'No, we just drove through.'
'It is worth a visit, sir. Close to there is a lake where they have the water for us to drink.'
'A reservoir?'
'That is it. Forgive my English.'
'Your English sounds very good to me,' she said.
'Thank you, Madame.'

'You don't sound Portuguese.'

'I am half French, Madame…Our house is close to the reservoir and the water there is very low. I walk with my dog there nearly every day…You are here on holiday?'

'Yes,' she smiled, knowing that he had not ignored her, even when she had not been speaking. 'We have come here to do nothing. Just relax.'

'That is wonderful, Madame. It is how it should be on holiday.'

'We have a little villa and pool on a lemon farm not far from here.'

He nodded, as though appreciating the seclusion offered by such a place.

'Far from the crowds,' he said. 'And you can come and go as you please.'

'Exactly,' she said. 'A chance to get away from it all for a time. We can sit and read for as long as we want. There is nobody putting pressure on us to do anything.'

'Last time we came,' her husband explained. 'There was always our son to consider. He wanted to go to the water parks and to the beaches and shopping, while all we wanted to do was sit and do nothing.'

'And now, with the two of you, you can do that.'

'Yes,' she said.

'It will be like a great weight has been taken from you?' he smiled. 'To escape from your everyday lives.'

'Yes,' her husband agreed. 'We're beginning to relax more, now that we are away from it all. Aren't we, love?'

'It has always seemed to me that life is like going to work,' the owner continued. 'You wake up and clock in and, just before you go to sleep, you clock out. It may be that real life is only in those moments between the clocking in and out.'

The waitress appeared. 'Your table is ready.'

She led them to a table by a window. Over the rooftops, they could see the sun touching the hills of Monchique, like a clot of congealing blood.

The meal was everything she had hoped for and the wine matched it sublimely. Why had no one joined them? Why were they the only guests? They had spent the whole evening alone in the restaurant, cocooned in its gentle light. Although she had enjoyed every moment, she had felt this nagging doubt that something was wrong. She wished that others would join them. It seemed so unfair that such a place should be passed by. How could the owner make a living if so few came? Yet the owner seemed unconcerned. It seemed that fate had decided that he would have only two guests that night and he took great pleasure in their company. They had discussed music and the great albums, or their favourite tracks that accompanied important moments in their lives. She had teased her husband with great delight when the owner had dismissed Chekhov as a world-weary bore, whose heroes were no better than the property owners in Guia, looking for a better life than their own in lands of dreams.

When they had finished the meal, he brought them coffee.

'Black for Madame and white for sir…And I have for you a special wine to go with the coffee.'

He poured the wine into the two liqueur glasses and

stepped back to watch them. She picked up the glass and sipped. The wine seemed to fill her mouth, her throat and then her whole being.
'What is this?' she gasped.
'It is a special wine I have for my guests, Madame.'
She heard her husband gasp with pleasure. The owner smiled and left them.
'This is fantastic, love,' he grinned.
'Just remember who's driving,' she warned.
'Do you want to come here again?'
'We have to!'
'Shall we book? It's going to be a bit more expensive than the others.'
'We have enough. Don't worry about the money.'
They drank their coffees and finished the wine. When the waitress returned to clear the table they asked for the bill. The owner appeared.
'Did you enjoy the wine?'
'We did indeed,' her husband enthused. 'In fact the whole evening has been fantastic.'
'It has been my pleasure, sir.'
'Could we book again?'
'Certainly, sir.'
'For two days time.'
'Yes, sir,' he smiled and left again.
When the waitress returned with the bill, it was not as much as they thought it would be. She seemed embarrassed by their generous tip. As they pushed aside the curtain to leave, the owner met them on the landing.
'Sir,' he said, apologetically. 'You have made a mistake and left too much.'
He handed them a twenty-euro note.

'That would be enough,' he said. 'Please take care as you go down the stairs and enjoy your two days together. I look forward to your return.'

'Well…Thank you,' they said, rather confused that some of their money should be returned. They stepped carefully down the stairway and out into the night.

It was not until they were in the car and driving back to the villa that they realised he had not taken their names.

As they drove along the track, they caught the shapes of two dogs bounding across the fields in the headlights. They pulled onto the steep driveway and he left the car in gear so that it would not roll backwards.

'Do you have the key?' he asked as he turned off the engine and the interior light came on.

She fumbled through her bag.

'Yes, they're here, love.'

They got out of the car. A pool of light waited for them by the doorway. He pressed the button on the remote and the lock clicked shut on the car. The interior light faded away into the dark. As they walked up the three steps to the patio, they could see the line of ants crossing the path, scaling the wall and continuing on their relentless journey to the drainage pipe that led to the garden below. She put the key in the lock.

'Now, remember. Three turns,' he said, trying to be helpful.

'I know. I know,' she said, slightly irritated by his reminder.

The key turned easily twice but then would go no further. She tutted, feeling a slight panic creeping into her air of confidence.

'Do you need to wiggle it?' he suggested.

'It's all right,' she said. 'I've got it.' She tried wiggling the key in the lock but it did not work. She could sense he was becoming annoyed and wanted to take control. She turned the key to lock the door and then tried again. One. Two. Three! The door opened.

'There you are!' she announced triumphantly.

He pushed gently past her, switched on the light and quickly entered the code. The alarm system bip-bipped and fell silent. He blew out his cheeks in relief.

'Sorry, love,' he said. 'I was panicking a bit.'

'Come here, you daft thing,' she said and put her arms around him. They hugged and embraced.

'I love you, you know,' he said.

'I know…And, after all these years, I still don't know why.'

'Because you're you.'

They kissed again.

'I tell you what,' she said. 'Let's have some of that Cointreau on the balcony, under the stars.'

'Great idea,' he grinned.

She got two glasses from the cupboard and opened the bottle, while he got the ice out of the freezer. She poured in the Cointreau and left the bottle on the top of the cupboard, not noticing the drops trickling slowly down the neck of the bottle. He dropped in the ice cube and, by the time he had closed the freezer, the Cointreau had turned to a ghostly white in the glass. They climbed the stairs, unlocked the door and stepped out onto the balcony. Across the fields they

could see the lights of two small houses and on the horizon the eerie glow of a distant town. Above them the sky was filled with stars. They sat in blissful silence and drank their chilled Cointreau. She gazed up at the night sky, trying to find Orion, the only constellation she could recognise, but it was not there. He had told her about the stars and how the Earth's movement through space made the heavens into some great timepiece, but she had never really understood. For her the sky had always meant heaven, just as her mother and grandmother had told her when she was a child. She knew what the scientists had said and their explanations about it all. The parts that she could follow seemed to make sense. But in her heart, in her soul, it had never felt right. This felt right. This moment beneath the stars of heaven and knowing she was part of it all felt right.
'Are you ready?' a voice called to her.
For a moment she was confused and then realised it must have been her husband's voice.
'Yes, love.'
'I'll take them down.'
He reached for her glass and she held onto his hand.
'You know I love you so much,' she said.
He smiled.
'Come on. Let's go in, before the mosquitoes get you.'
She went to the bedroom and undressed, while he took the glasses downstairs to the kitchen and returned to go to the bathroom. She listened to him cleaning his teeth and waited in the bedroom while he urinated. When she heard him flush the toilet she got up from the bed and went to the landing. The wine and

Cointreau were making her feel light-headed. He opened the door.
'Are you okay?' he asked, looking concerned.
'Yes, I'm fine.'
She went into the bathroom and closed the door. The light over the mirror was far too harsh. She cleaned her teeth and spat into the sink. There was a faint trace of blood. She rinsed out her mouth, wiped her lips on the towel and noticed the fresh pink stain. She placed the towel over the side of the bath, switched off the light and closed the door. Leaving the landing light on, a habit she had kept from childhood, she returned to the bedroom.
'I'll need to go to the dentist when we get back,' she said.
He looked up from his Chekhov.
'What's wrong?'
'My gums must be bleeding.'
She got into bed and lay on her side, facing him. The fan was blowing cool air across the bed.
'Are you going to read?'
'No. I was just waiting for you.'
He took off his glasses and lay down beside her.
'Thank you for tonight,' she whispered.
He lay on his back, his eyes closed.
'I loved it,' he said. 'Just you and me.'
She waited. He just lay there.
'I'll see you in the morning,' she sighed and turned over, resigning herself to sleep.
She felt him move as he turned on to his side. And then, to her great joy, he gently touched her breast. She felt a great thrill run through her body and she turned back to face him.

Downstairs a trail of ants had found the remains of the Cointreau and was exploring the empty glasses left on the side.

When she woke in the morning, she knew that she had slept well. They lay in bed together and let the fan blow the cool air over them. They laughed and teased each other, as they had done when young lovers. Eventually, she persuaded him to shower first and pushed him out of bed. He grabbed a pillow and threw it at her.
'Just because you can't win!' she laughed, as he went down the stairs.
She heard him turn on the downstairs lights and then open one of the shutters to let in the sunlight. Suddenly he cursed and called to her.
'What's the matter?'
'Come and look at this.'
'If this is one of your tricks to get me out of bed…'
'No, come and look.'
She heard him continuing to curse and knew something was wrong. She got out of bed and put on her nightdress.
'What's wrong?' she asked, as she made her way down. The tiles were cold on her feet.
'We've got those bloody ants again!'
He was searching for the spray.
'It's under the sink,' she said. 'I didn't want it near the food.'
She saw the trail over the work surface leading to the base of the bottle.
'Look at them,' he nodded towards the glasses, which seemed strangely dark. She then realised that they were

covered in ants.

'Sorry, love,' he apologised. 'I left them out last night. I should have put them in the bowl of water.'

'You can't spray them.'

'I know.'

He picked up a glass with his fingertips and took it over to the bowl. As the glass sank into the soapy water, the ants floated on the surface like a black scum. While she looked on in horror, he did the same with the second glass and then poured the water down the sink. Some of the ants' remains seem to congeal in the sink. He ran the hot water and flushed them away.

'I'll go for a shower,' she said.

'You don't have to.'

He began to spray the tops of the cupboards and she could feel the poison in her throat.

'No, it's okay,' she said and escaped into the shower room.

It was while they were reading, having finished their light breakfast, that she suddenly announced, 'Why don't we go to Silves today?'

'We could do,' he answered, a little surprised. 'I thought you just wanted to read today.'

'I thought it would be different. We didn't see it before.'

'Fine,' he said. 'I'll get the map.'

She cleared away and he studied the map.

'It's easy, really,' he called. 'Just along the motorway.'

'I'll get some money from the safe,' she said. 'Just in case.'

They put on the alarm and locked the villa.

'They're still asleep,' she said, as they passed the dogs.

Reaching Silves was easy. They found the narrow road that led to the fortress and parked beneath the shade of the church. Finding the entrance to the fort was more difficult. There seemed to be no way in at first. However much they tried, the path seemed to end with them facing the huge statue of a famous Christian knight, who had died long ago. They were about to give up when they caught sight of some people. Following them, the entrance seemed to appear from nowhere and they could not believe they had not found the way already. Once inside, they could see the painting, which showed an interpretation of how the great fortress had been in the time of the Moors. Now the plan was to restore it to its original magnificent beauty. They wandered inside and saw that the fortress was just a ruin. The outside walls remained in all their splendour, like a huge protective shell. From the towers were wonderful views of the valley and its surrounding hills, but, inside the walls, all that remained were the base stones of buildings destroyed long ago. As they walked around the walls, they could see the evidence of all the work that was being done to try to bring life back into the citadel. With the sun beating down on them, they felt trapped between a dream of the past and a dream of the future.

On the way back they left the motorway and took the road to Pera. As they drove along the quiet road they saw signs for an exhibition of sand sculptures.

'It's on this road,' he said. 'Do you want to call in and see what it's like?'

'You can do,' she replied and he could still feel her disappointment.

The dusty car park was easy to find and they parked alongside the few cars that were already there. They had to cross the road to get in to the exhibition, which seemed to be held in the middle of nowhere. They had seen sand sculptures on beaches before and expected to see the usual array of mermaids and dolphins. What they did see amazed them. Huge banks of sculptures portraying ancient civilisations and scenes from prehistoric times seem to envelope them. At each exhibit they stood in awe at the size of the figures and the detail shaped in the fine grains of sand. Scenes from ancient Egypt, India, China and Mexico. And, amongst it all, she saw the head of Buddha, sculpted into a great bank. She stared at, transfixed by the serenity the sculptor had captured in the sand. She stared and could see that all of this seemed to emanate from him like a great dream. Not just the sand sculptures but the whole place. And, standing before him, she knew that she was part of it all.
'How did they get it all here?' she heard her husband asking from a distance.
'All this sand,' he continued. 'Where did they get it from? We're in the middle of nowhere, or it must just be someone's field. So how did they get it here?'
She felt the moment pass and saw him with his camera.
'I don't know, love,' she smiled.
'It's incredible, isn't it?'
'Absolutely!'
'How do they get it to stay together for so long?'
He reached out to touch.
'No! Don't touch it!'
It was too late. Part of the sculpture crumbled away.
'Now look what happened!'

'I was just...'

'I know,' she said. 'But you shouldn't have disturbed it.'

'I thought it must be sprayed with something to keep it together.'

'Come on, let's go.'

'Well, why doesn't it just blow away or collapse?' he persisted as they made their way back to the car.

'Perhaps there's something special holding it all together,' was all that she could say.

When they arrived back at the villa, having passed the sleeping dogs, she prepared a light meal of fruit, cheese and bread. They ate by the pool and read for a while. Her mind seemed to be elsewhere and, no matter how much she tried, she could not get into her book. She tried to lie back in the sun but it was no use.

'I think I'll go in the pool,' she said.

'I'll just finish this part,' he said and touched her hand as she passed.

In the bedroom she undressed and let the fan blow the cool air over her. She felt it between her legs and lifted her breasts to let it evaporate the sweat that lay hidden beneath. She put on her costume and it felt uncomfortable against her. Collecting her towel from the bed, she went down to the pool. He had just finished reading.

'I won't be long,' he called as he climbed the stairs.

She entered the pool and let the water take her body into its cool embrace. Once it had reached her shoulders she removed the straps to her costume and rolled it down to her waist. She turned on to her back and swam to the deep end, watching the blue sky above her. Holding onto the side, she waited for him to return. He threw his towel over the rail and gingerly came down the steps into the shallow end. She let him splash the water over his shoulders and swam towards him, as he walked to the middle of the pool.

'What are you doing?' he gasped, as he saw her semi nakedness.

'It's all right,' she said. 'It doesn't matter. No one can see.'

'What if someone comes?'

'I can easily cover myself.'

She floated by the side of him and could see he was secretly delighted.

'It's lovely,' she teased and swam off.

'Well, I never thought I'd see the day…' he laughed, as he swam after her.

They swam and floated together for some time. She leant her back against him and he held her naked breasts while she floated beside him, happy to be alone with him. Suddenly she turned and said, 'Shall we go inside?'

He smiled and they got out of the pool, the water falling from them. They began to dry themselves in the sun and removed their costumes. In the kitchen they dried each other with gentle strokes and caresses. Leaving their towels, they climbed the stairs to lie in bed together and let the cool air from the fan blow over them in the heat of the late afternoon.

When they awoke, he noticed the mark.

'What's that?' he asked, a slight panic in his voice.

'What?'

'On your breast.'
He touched her and pressed against her breast.
'There's a dark mark.'
She sat up and felt herself.
'I can't feel anything,' she said. 'It doesn't hurt and there's no lump.'
'It doesn't look like a bruise.'
She got out of bed and went to the mirror in the bathroom. There was mark beneath the fold of her breast, like a dark stain.
'It's nothing,' she assured him, when she returned to the bedroom.
'We need to keep an eye on it,' he insisted.
'I'll go to the doctors when we get back,' she said.
She picked up a clean towel and could see the worry on his face.
'Don't worry,' she said. 'There's no lump. I probably knocked into something.'
She left the room and called back to him, 'Besides, it'll give you a reason to examine them every day!'
'You saucy devil!' he shouted.
He listened to her getting into the shower and lay down on the bed, trying not to worry.
She stood in the heat of the shower, trying to remember.

After showering and getting dressed he came down the stairs and she was ready to go.
'I thought we'd try phoning again,' she said. 'Are you ready?'
'Yes,' he said, feeling a little confused. 'Where do you want to eat?'
'We're going to the Casa.'

'That's tomorrow.'
'No. It's tonight.'
'Are you sure…I thought we booked it for tomorrow? Didn't we say in two days?'
'Yes…and that's today.'
'Today?'
'Yes.'
'But I thought we only booked it yesterday?'
'No…that was two days ago.'
He tried to remember what they had done yesterday.
'I don't remember yesterday…'
'You do. We went out to Silves.'
'I thought that was today.'
'No…that was yesterday…Don't you remember?'
'What did we do today?'
'Nothing. You wanted to go to Albufeira but we stayed here.'
'I honestly don't remember, love…Are you sure.'
'Yes, of course I am…Look, come on. We're going to be late. And you hate being late.'
They secured the villa and left. The dogs were standing and seemed much larger than before. Their eyes were closed.

When they reached Guia, he turned into their usual car park and found a space. He stopped and put the car into reverse. There was a sudden whining noise and the car lurched backwards.
'What the..!' he shouted and pressed hard onto the brake. The car kept moving. He pressed again and turned the wheel to avoid a car parked behind him.
'What are you doing?' she cried.
'I'm trying to stop this…'

He slammed his foot against the pedal and held it down. He could feel the brake discs straining against the pads. He pressed and pressed but the car continued on its slow, inevitable journey. He grabbed the handbrake and pulled as hard as he could. The car stopped centimetres from the granite embankment. He switched off the ignition and collapsed against the steering wheel, exhausted.
'Are you all right?'
'Yes,' he gasped. 'I think so...'
'What on earth happened?'
'I have no idea...It just suddenly...'
'Is it safe?'
'I've switched the engine off.'
'I know...but is it safe to drive?'
He sat up and turned on the ignition. The engine sparked into life and he put it into gear. He drove slightly forward and stopped. It was fine. Taking a deep breath, he put it into reverse. The car behaved perfectly.
'It seems fine now,' he said and turned off the engine.
They got out, locked the car and walked to the phone box. She searched through her purse and took out a euro. She lifted the receiver, listened and pushed the coin into the slot.
'You put the number in this time,' she insisted.
He leaned in and methodically punched in the number. She stood with the receiver pressed against her ear.
'It's ringing,' she said and put her finger into her other ear to mask the sound of the passing traffic. Suddenly she heard her son's voice, 'Hello?'
'Hello, love. It's mum,' she called. 'Are you all right? We couldn't get through 'til now.'

'Hello?' the voice repeated.
'Hello, love. It's mum…It must be this terrible traffic…Can you hear me?'
'Hello?'
'I'm just phoning to say we're all right!' she shouted.
'Hello?'
'There's something wrong here,' she said, handing him the phone. 'He can't hear me…You try.'
He squeezed past her. When he put the receiver to his ear there was nothing but the empty buzz of a dead line.
'Hello?' he called, hopefully. But there was no answer. He replaced the receiver.
'No one there.'
'How are we going to let him know that we're okay?' she asked.
'Try again tomorrow,' he said.
They crossed the road and walked up the hill through the village. As before the Casa seemed to show no sign of life until they had passed through the curtain and found the owner sitting on the large terrace.
'Please, forgive me,' he said in that quiet voice. 'I was reading.'
He closed his book and smiled.
'You are most welcome again…'
He moved a table for them and they sat down.
'No one here again!'
'No, sir. It is most strange…Yesterday was busy but…Perhaps it is the crossing over time. Some tourists leave today and new ones arrive…What can I get for you, Madame? It was a Sauvignon Blanc, was it not?'
'Yes, please,' she smiled delighted that he had remembered.

'And a soft drink for you, sir?'
'Yes, please.'
'I will leave you with the menu…'
It was as though she had never left. Everything felt just right and she knew that the meal, the whole experience, would be just as wonderful as it had been before.

They sat at the same table and gazed out at the blood-red sun suspended between the oncoming darkness and the shadow it cast across the earth. They were alone. The owner came to their table as before and made them feel at ease. It was at the end of the main course that her husband asked, 'When we came, yesterday…No, sorry, not yesterday…When we were here before you said life could be like clocking on and off…Like going to work.'
'For many of us, sir, work seems to dominate our whole being. Each day we feel more and more exhausted by the tasks that life seems to set down for us. We long for sleep and yet, when that sleep comes it is filled with bad dreams and, when we wake…Our lives and dreams seem to drain all our life force from us.'
'And the moments between?' her husband asked, trying to understand.
'Are our chances to recharge ourselves.'
'Like our holidays,' she said.
'Yes.'
'But you weren't talking about holidays, were you?' her husband persisted.
She could see that the owner was not sure that he should continue.

'Have you lain awake at night, sir? Waiting for sleep to come?'

'Yes, we have all done that.'

'Doesn't it seem strange how one moment you are awake and the next in a dream that can feel more real than life itself and in between are those moments when we are neither awake nor dreaming.'

'When we are asleep.'

'But not dreaming…'

'You mean unconscious?'

'It is a strange time when you are not conscious…'

'But you are just asleep,' she said.

'Yes, Madame,' he smiled.

'I hardly ever remember my dreams,' she said.

'Except about the crocodiles trying to get you,' her husband laughed.

'Some say that, when we dream, it is like the soul is free to roam the world and to remember its previous lives,' the owner continued.

'That would mean you believe in reincarnation,' he said. 'And the duality of soul and body.'

'I wonder why I never remember my dreams?' she asked. 'I must dream…Everybody does…Don't they say we have to dream to keep ourselves sane?'

'Yes, Madame.'

'And do you believe that the soul goes to heaven when we die?' she asked him.

The owner smiled.

'Because you don't, do you, love?'

She turned accusingly to her husband. She knew what his answer would be and that his cold logic filled her with dread.

'I think we go back to the great nothing from where

we came,' he said, embarrassed by the chill he had brought into the room. 'I don't know what I was before I was born and I don't know what I will be when I die. I can only assume that it will be the same as before I was alive.'

'And I believe we go to heaven!' she said emphatically.

'Yes, love.'

'A friend once said to me that death was the only true experience,' the owner broke in.

'And what did you say?' she asked, a strange fear fluttering inside her.

He smiled, as though remembering the moment, and said, 'We were drinking at the time…and I hit him.'

'Hit him?'

'Yes, Madame…It seemed to be the right thing to do…to test his theory…'

'And what did he do?'

'At first he was shocked…I had not hit him hard but…he laughed, Madame. We both laughed…and then we had an argument about whether the experience had been his dream or mine…That was a long time ago.'

'And what do you think now?'

'I think it is time for your coffee, Madame,' he laughed.

They had their coffee and the special wine and asked for the bill.

'I hope everything was to your liking?' the owner smiled.

'Most enjoyable,' he said. 'Could we book again?'

'Of course, sir.'

'The next time may be our last because we are leaving.'

'In which case I will see that the meal is a special one for you.'

'That would be very kind.'
'My pleasure, sir.'
He pulled the curtain aside for them.
'Please take care on the stairway and have a safe journey home.'

They did not speak to each other on the way back in the car and did not see the two dogs. He brought a glass of Cointreau to her on the balcony.
'Are you all right?' he asked.
'Yes, love…just tired.'
'I haven't done something to upset you, have I?'
'No, of course not…I'm just tired.'
They sat in silence and drank the Cointreau. He knew there was something wrong and that there was nothing he could do.
'I'm going to go in then,' he said. 'Are you coming?'
'Not yet.'
'I'll go down and wash the glasses.'
He took her glass and left her. She looked up at the night sky and felt herself being drawn into its vastness. She closed her eyes. For some strange reason, she suddenly thought of the painting they had seen together on their last holiday in Paris. They had visited the Museum d'Orsay and found Courbet's 'Origin of the World'. She had been shocked at first. How could a woman allow someone to paint such a stark piece of her private life? He, of course, thought the painting a thing of great beauty and had talked about a sentence he had read in an article by Sigmund Freud. Something about how many of us object to the fact we are born between urine and faeces. She had been disgusted by the idea but knew that it was true. She laughed to

herself and thought, 'Him and his books. Always reading. Always searching…Tomorrow I will shock him. I will bathe naked in the pool and let him lift me, so that I can float in the water beneath the sky.' And then she heard the voice.

'Are you ready now?'

She opened her eyes and saw her father, who had died some years before. He was standing by her husband's chair.

'I need to go down to him,' she said, a slight panic rushing through her heart.

She hurried inside and locked the balcony door behind her. She called his name but there was no answer.

She went carefully down the stairs, trying not to fall and saw him sitting on the settee. She knew that he had gone. She sat beside him and leaned against him. They had been married for thirty years and she still loved him and this was where she wanted to be, safe by his side, always. She smiled, closed her eyes and waited for the dream to begin. A trail of ants crossed the tiled floor.

Each morning the two dogs would wake from their dream of freedom and find themselves tied to the tree.

They were found next to each other in their hire car. The police report said that they had swerved to miss a dog that had roamed onto the dual carriageway. In doing so, they had clipped the side of an oncoming lorry. Their car had careered across the road, smashed through a barrier, rolled several times and ended up in the field by a tree. They had died before an ambulance

WITH COMPLIMENTS:

Mathom House Publishing is a small, independent publisher, dedicated to well made, real books, with good paper…

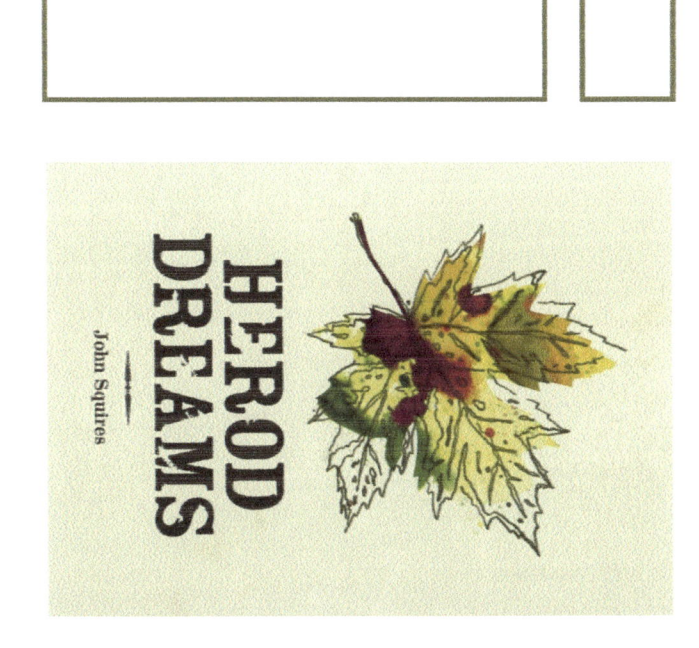

Book cutting
I hope you like it
John

Mathom House Publishing
152 Carter Lane East
South Normanton
Alfreton
Derbyshire
DE55 2DZ

john@johnpearce.org.uk
Telephone and fax: 01773 778013
Mobile 07972892807

HEROD DREAMS
John Squires

could reach them. The force of the crash had sealed the doors to the car and firemen had had to cut into it to release the bodies. In the time it had taken, ants from the field had already got to them. Their bodies were taken from the car and sealed in two thick, black bags. Two people joined together on a journey from one dream to another…

Their son was contacted and came to identify the bodies. He stood in the semi-dark and watched the man pull back the heavy zip of each black bag to reveal his mother and his father. It was then he knew that any dream or plan he had cherished in his heart had been taken by the will of God. And so...

Herod wept.

2

I was there when my mother died. I heard her last breath. I was sitting with my father, watching television. It was nearly two in the morning. At least I think it was. I can't be sure. I'm never any good at remembering detail. You'd have to ask my brothers. They would know. Anyway, it had been my turn to stay at the hospital and I was watching some baseball game and my father was asleep in the chair.
She had her own room. She had been there for about five days. My father had woken up in the morning and could not wake her. He had called the ambulance and they had rushed her to hospital, where they discovered a massive brain tumour. It had been a stroke and she was in a coma.
She had been ill for some time and no one had known what was wrong. They had examined her lungs, her stomach, her bowel but never her head. Why would they need to check her head? She had never complained of a headache.
I think it was one of my brothers who said that she was not to die alone. That one of us had to be there all the time. And we knew he was right. We agreed to take it in turns to stay overnight so that there would always be someone with her. They had said that, even though she was in a coma, she could hear us. And so we talked. Talked about nothing. I can't remember what we talked about. You would have to ask my brothers.
There were times when she would move her arm.

Raise it up into the air and someone would hold her hand and ask her what it was that she wanted. Each time my father would say that she was coming round. He'd want to call the nurse. Tell her that she was conscious.

'Squeeze my hand if you can hear me,' one of us would say. But nothing would happen. When I spoke to my wife about it, she said that, perhaps, my mother was reaching to touch heaven or, perhaps, her body was trying to hold on to her soul.

At the beginning we would use the plastic sticks with small sponges on the end to wet her mouth. You could feel her clenching her gums and sucking on the end of the stick.

'She's sucking,' we would say. 'That's a good sign.'

During the day relatives and friends would visit and that would allow you some time to wander the corridors alone. After they had offered their best wishes, made polite conversations and told us all to take care, they would leave. Only one person broke down and sobbed in front of her. At least as far as I can remember.

Grandchildren came to see their grandma but did not know what to say or do. The looks on their fathers' faces made them afraid.

At night we would sit in silence and listen to her breathe. The small talk of the day had been all used up and there was nothing left to say. One of us would sit and keep awake, while the other tried to sleep in a chair. I could never sleep. I would try to read but it would be no use. That's why I turned on the television. I can't remember who was with me at the time. In fact, I think I was by myself. Yes, when I try to picture it, I can remember saying, 'Do you mind if I put the television on, mum?' It might have seemed almost sacrilegious, to do such a thing, at such a time. But the television was always on in her house. She would always be watching it. And so, at night, we would have the television on and talk to her about each programme. For me it helped to ease the time of her dying. I couldn't sleep and couldn't dream and so I let the television do the dreaming for me.

The next morning one of my brothers would return. We would talk about the night and the arrangements for the next day. Sometimes I would stay until the afternoon and then go home to sleep.

I could not bring myself to sleep at my parents' house and so would drive fifty miles home to my family. I would arrive exhausted and talk again about the night and how grandma was all right. There had been no change and that was a good sign.

In the bedroom I would hug my wife. Hold her so tight! Although my head was filled with the dread of the present moment and the moment in the future that we knew was bound to come, I did not cry. When I slept, my dreams filled me with fear. I woke and showered and ate and drove back to the room.

And all of this began to feel like a dream. In the fog of exhaustion, it was as though I was part of a film or a book or any one of those things that we have created for our dreaming. The days and nights with my mother seem to merge into a long moment of waiting.

And then her breathing changed. I think I felt it first rather than heard it. Anyway, something made me stop watching the television and I knew it was beginning to happen. I went to the side of her bed and I could tell. My father was asleep in the chair. I called him and went to get the nurse. When we returned, he was holding her hand.

The nurse went to the side of the bed. I could tell by her face that the time was near. 'I think you need to call your brothers,' she said. 'She is very close now.'

I heard my father cry, as I went out to the telephone. It was about two fifteen, I think. You would have to check with my brothers. They would remember the time.

The television was still on when I went back into the room. It was stupid of me to leave it like that. I sat by the side of her bed and, from somewhere deep inside, something heaved itself into being. No matter how much I tried, I could not choke it back. I sobbed and tears flooded down my face.

And then I heard someone on the television say that someone in some baseball team had scored a home run and the tears stopped and the dreaming seemed to begin again…

"What went ye out into
the wilderness to see?"

The dream of the father…

"Holy, holy, holy…"

Sanctus

1

I was not blessed with the birth of a son.
If he had come into the world, I dream of the life he would have lived and the path he would have taken. I would not want it to be like mine. I would not leave him, as my father left me. I would not forsake him. I would not want his body to be like mine, weak and full of temptation. I would not want him to look at himself in the mirror and feel the shame of self-doubt that corrodes my spirit. I would not have him witness the same brutality and horror that had driven me to find meaning in my wilderness of dead philosophers and sages. I would want him be confident in his own being. I would want his life filled with the joy of living. I would want him to go out into the world and be part of it.
But I know that I am just dreaming. I know that, if he had been born into this world, he would have been driven into his own wilderness. And, once there, he could only survive on his strength of will. And I would pray that not a bone of him would be broken and that his body would not be full of darkness.
But I know that I am only dreaming. I know that his life will end, betrayed by friends and strangers. His hands and feet will be crushed and his side pierced. And I know that his broken body will cry out to me, 'Father, behold thy son!'

2

And on a Saturday he would go out into the world of strangers to collect their money. Newspapers would be delivered to their houses and it was his job to collect their due payment. He would walk their streets and knock on their doors. For most people he was only the boy who came for the paper money and the time spent with him only a moment to pay for the bad news they had been reading all week. But for some, his coming was a blessed moment to talk to someone who seemed to listen, a chance to meet with a stranger.

And on one street there was a man who knew his father. They had been friends before the war. When his father had crossed the sea to fight for his country, his friend had stayed to work in the mines. Both men had shared time with the dead and the dying. His father on the fields of war, and his father's friend beneath the ground, where a collapse would seal men into the darkness and they would wait and hope for rescue, clinging to the will to live as the air became poisoned by their own breath.

Now his father's friend had been blessed with a gift. He could paint pictures of animals so well that they looked as though they were alive. He seemed to capture their very essence on his canvas. People would bring their pets to him and he would paint them with ease. The owners would be amazed. Such a likeness was better than any photograph. His work helped to pay the bills but filled his heart with great sadness, for in each portrait he knew he had caught sight of a trapped soul yearning for its wild ancestors. His great joy was to paint a creature from the wild. He would sit for hours and watch the birds in his garden. He would journey into the countryside in the hope of glimpsing a wild deer. He would visit zoos and return with sketches of lost souls.

And, each Saturday, his father's friend would invite the boy into his kitchen.

'Come in, youth,' he would say. 'You must have a thirst on yer. Tek off yer sack an' sit yer sen down.'

His wife would smile and bring a mug of tea.

'Ow's yer father?' he would ask and they would talk of the week, and of his father's work, and of his mother's sorrows and of his studies.

'You kep on with them studies,' he would say. 'Yer father is right proud of you, youth. Oh, I know he don't say nowt to you, but he talks about yer all the time.'

And when the time came for him to go, his father's friend would bring out his latest painting.

'What yer think?' he would ask.

It might be a great cat, dreaming of the plains, a hawk, dreaming of the sky or a great ape, dreaming of its freedom.

'All of 'em have souls, yer know,' he would say. 'All on 'em. Just look in their eyes an' yer can tell.'

'It's wonderful,' he would say.

Now one day the boy went to his father's friend and asked for a favour. On the wall in the kitchen was a portrait of the man's wife and the boy knew that his father's friend had painted it. When he had asked about it, the man had told him that this was a painting he treasured more than any other, for it showed his wife as she always was and always would be, no matter what the world and time would do to her. And he asked the man if he would paint a portrait of his father. It was to be his father's birthday soon and he wanted to give him something special, to show how much he loved him. His father's friend sighed and seemed to hesitate.

'Are yer sure yer father would want it?'

The boy looked at the portrait of the man's wife. He was sure.

'I have a photograph of him,' he said. 'Of when he was younger.'

'I'll not need no photo, youth,' he said.

'I'll pay you,' the boy said.

'No, youth,' he said. 'No need. It's a gift.'

'Let me pay for the materials.'

'Fair enough.'

The man looked hard at the boy.

'You are sure about this gift?' he asked.

'Yes, I'm sure.'

They agreed upon a price and the man set to work.

On the day before his father's birthday the portrait was finished. The man had wrapped it to protect it from the rain that fell.

'Do yer not want to look at it before yer tek it?' the man asked.

'No,' the boy said. It would be a shame to break open the wrapping.

The package was smaller than the boy had thought. He carried it carefully home, protecting it against the driving rain that seemed to want to snatch it from him.

That night he could hardly sleep, his heart filled with the excitement of presenting his father with such a gift. In the morning he placed the package by the side of his father's chair and waited for him to come down.

His father opened his cards and smiled. Then he reached for the package.

'What's this then?' he laughed.

'It's for you,' the boy said.

His father tore the wrapping away. For a moment he looked at the portrait and then seemed to change. He threw it to the floor, covered his face with his hands and began to cry. The boy was horrified. What was wrong? He looked at the portrait that lay on the floor. It looked like his father, an exact likeness. Then what was wrong? What had his father seen?

'What's up, love?' his mother asked.

She had never seen her husband cry before. She picked up the painting and gasped. There, before her, was the face of the man she loved and in his eyes she saw the horror that tortured his very soul.

3

And on the same street there lived a fool and his dog. And the fool and his dog would wait for the boy each day. And, when the boy did not return, the fool would run to his mother and cry, 'He has not come! The boy has not returned!' And his mother would explain that the boy did not come every day but only on special days. And the fool would ask, 'Will the boy come tomorrow?' And his mother would explain that it was only on a Saturday that the boy appeared. And the fool would ask, 'Is tomorrow Saturday? Is tomorrow the special day?' And his mother would explain that sometimes tomorrow would be Saturday, but often he would have to wait for a tomorrow and tomorrow and tomorrow before the special day would arrive. And so, his head full of tomorrows, the fool and his dog would stand and wait by his gate, hoping the boy would come.

And each Saturday, the boy would arrive and the fool would laugh out loud, clap his hands and shout, 'You have come! I knew you would come!' And the fool would race to his mother to tell her the good news. 'He has come! The one we were waiting for has come!' And his mother, the fool and the dog dancing around her, would come to the gate with her purse and say to her son, 'Do you want to pay the boy our dues?' And the fool would grin and say, 'Yes, mother. I will pay the boy.' And the mother would take the correct money from her purse and hand it to her child, saying, 'Here you are. Make sure it's the right amount.' And the fool would step towards the boy and bow his head and say, 'I will pay you.' And he would carefully press

each silver coin into the boy's hand and count. And, when he had reached the final piece of silver, he would say, 'There, I have paid you our dues.' And he would step back and bow. And the boy would place the coins in the bag and thank them. And the fool would ask, 'Will you come again?' And the boy would say, 'Yes, I will come again.' And the fool would ask, 'Will it be tomorrow?' And his mother would hold his hand and say, 'No, my love. It's on Saturday…Remember?'
Now, one day, the boy arrived at the fool's gate and the fool was waiting as usual with the dog. In his hand he held a long bamboo cane.
'This is for you,' the fool said and passed the long bamboo cane over the gate.
'Well, thank you,' the boy said, confused by the gift.
'Can you make it work?' the fool asked.
The boy was trying to understand the foolishness he was being drawn into.
'What's wrong with it?' he asked, feeling the weight of it in his hand.
'It doesn't work.'
'What doesn't it do?'
'It doesn't reach.'
'What?'
'You need to fix it for me.'
'What are you trying to reach?'
'Heaven.'
The boy felt a sudden rush of panic and could not speak.
'My father said that heaven is behind the stars and I tried to touch it with my stick, but I couldn't reach. I climbed as high as I could but it was no good.'
'Did you tell your father?'

'Yes.'
'What did he say?'
'He said that heaven was where we go when we die and that I was not dead and I could not kill myself to reach heaven because if I killed myself I would not go to heaven. God would know and send me to hell. And I asked him how I could reach heaven and he said that I could reach heaven through Jesus and he would come to me if I prayed to him and I prayed to him and he told me to give the stick to you and you would make the stick reach heaven for me…'
The dog jumped up at the gate and barked, expecting the boy to do something.
'Is your mum in?'
'Yes.'
'Can you get her for me?'
'Yes.'
The fool stood on the other side of the gate, waiting.
'Can you go and get her now?'
'Can you fix the stick now?' the fool asked hopefully.
'Not at the moment…'
'And will you return with it mended?'
'One day…'
'Shall I get my mother?'
'Yes, please.'
The fool raced away to the back of his house followed by the dog, while the boy stood by the gate holding his unwanted gift. No matter how he tried, he could not think clearly. His mind was trapped in a world of foolishness. When the fool and his mother appeared, he was still at the gate clutching the long bamboo cane.
'And what have we here?' the fool's mother asked.
'He is going to mend my heaven stick,' the fool smiled.

'Oh, I see,' said his mother and took out the pieces of silver for her son to pay to the boy.

'Now check that carefully before you give it to him,' she said to her son and winked at the boy. As the fool sorted through the coins in his hands, his mother reached over to take the cane from the boy.

'Well, thank you very much!' she called out in delight. The fool looked up from his concentration. 'Look what he's done for you!' his mother beamed. The fool grinned and reached for the cane.

'No. We must pay him first!' she scolded. The fool counted out the silver and his mother passed the cane to him.

'Now, what must he do for the stick to work? Ah, yes. At night, when the stars shine bright, you must close your eyes, hold your breath and reach high into the sky. And, if you've been a good boy, the stick will stretch and stretch right past the moon, right past the stars until it reaches heaven. And, if you keep your eyes closed and keep your faith, you will feel heaven and see it in your heart…Isn't that right?' She turned and looked at the boy.

'Yes,' he said. 'That's right.'

'Thank you,' said the fool. 'Thank you. Thank you.'

The fool's mother smiled at the boy and held her son's hand.

'Can we try it tonight?' he asked.

'That depends on whether the stars are out,' she said, leading him along the path.

4

And there was at the end of his round an old woman living in a small house, whose garden overlooked the river. And the boy would have to cross the bridge to the other side to call on the woman. Now one day, the boy was caught in a sudden storm. The sky was dark when he reached the woman's door. He stood in her doorway, soaked by the rain. She was a kind woman and let him take shelter while the storm passed. She offered him a drink and they stood together in her kitchen, waiting for the sky to clear. Through her kitchen window he saw the sun burst from behind a cloud and flood her garden with light. For a moment it took his breath away. It seemed such a beautiful place, filled with flowers and small fruit trees. When the storm had passed, the old woman took him into her garden and explained that her husband had looked after it for many years and that, now he had passed away, she was afraid it would turn into a wilderness again. The boy wandered through the garden in the pleasant shade and listened to the old woman as she named the plants and touched the trees. He felt himself overwhelmed by the different colours and fragrances, by the sounds of the birds in the trees. As they followed each path, they would turn a corner and the boy would gasp in awe, as another part of the garden was revealed.

After some time, they reached the end of the garden and before them stood a tall mound and hewn from the mound was a small shelter, within which there lay a slab of rock. The old woman explained that the shelter had been used by her son many years before. He would use it as a place of rest, while his father worked in the garden. But that was long ago, before he had become a doctor and left to make a new start on the other side of the world.

Above the mound was a tall hedge. A great tangle of thorns wrapped itself around it and stretched out onto the mound beneath. The old woman explained that it was this part of the garden that she could no longer control. The wilderness threatened to creep from the hedge and cover her son's place of rest.

The boy agreed to help the old woman. He would return each Sunday and work on the mound. He would take no money for the work but the old woman would provide him with food and drink.

When the boy returned on the first Sunday the old woman had found her husband's gloves and tools. It was a fine day and the boy welcomed the shade of the trees as he set to work. He placed the old man's gloves and tools onto the slab of rock and took out some gloves and a pair of secateurs he had brought from his own house. He had borrowed them from his father. It was not that they were better than the old man's. It was just that he felt uncomfortable wearing a dead man's gloves and using his tools. He climbed the mound and began to cut away at the green stems. As he worked, loose soil and stones tumbled down the mound and clattered into the shelter below. He cut steadily and patiently, throwing the severed stems and branches onto the grass beneath. As he cut deeper into the hedge, he disturbed the dust, that had collected on the leaves, and his sweat turned it into grime on his skin. The thorns turned from green to dry brown, as he cut his way into the woody core. The gloves protected his hands but the thorns about his head marked him. He was so absorbed by his task he did not feel the pain and thought the blood trickling down his face was only sweat. He had worked for more than an hour, when the old lady called to him from the garden.

'Hello! I'm making some tea…I thought we could sit in the garden.'

She appeared at the base of the mound.

'How is it going? You appear to have done a lot already.'

He pulled out a knot of thorns from the hedge and turned to smile at her.

'What on earth have you done to your head?'

Instinctively he touched his forehead.

'No! Don't touch. It will make it worse.'

He looked at the gloves and saw the dark stain on its fingertips.

'You're bleeding,' she said. 'Come down and I'll look at it for you.'

'It'll be all right,' he said, embarrassed by the fuss.

'No, it won't,' she insisted. 'Come down. It needs cleaning or it will go septic.'

He scrambled down and followed her back to the house.

In the kitchen she made him sit down while she found a clean cloth and poured some hot water from the kettle into a bowl. She let the cloth settle into the hot water and searched for some antiseptic cream.

'I need to wash your face,' she said, as though asking for permission. 'Ah, here it is.'

She took out a small tube from a cupboard.

He realised he was still wearing the gloves and pulled

them off. The inner lining rubbed against his sweat-softened fingers.

'I'm sorry,' he said.

'Don't be silly…Here. This will stop your shirt getting wet.'

She placed a towel over his chest and shoulders.

'And you can use it to dry yourself when we've finished.'

She took the cloth from the bowl and squeezed out the excess water.

'Head back,' she said. 'And close your eyes.'

He leant back so that his head rested on the back of the chair.

'I'll try not to hurt,' she whispered.

He felt the gentle heat of the wet cloth on his head.

'Does that hurt?'

'No. That's fine.'

'You must tell me if it does.'

She pressed the cloth against the wounds, letting the warm water lift the drying blood from his skin. He felt trails of cooling water run through his hair.

'Keep your head still,' she said and he felt the weight of the cloth lifted from him.

He heard her wash out the cloth in the bowl and listened to the sound of the water.

'Ready?' she asked.

'Yes,' he said and again the cloth was laid on his head.

'Please, tell me if it hurts.'

As the old woman bathed his head and washed the grime from his face, he felt the water draw the pain from his wounds and cleanse the blood from his skin. All too soon she had completed her gentle healing and began to dry his forehead.

'That's better,' she said. 'You're clean now. I just need to put on the cream. You can open your eyes now.'

He opened his eyes as though awakening from a deep sleep. She smiled at him and, for a moment he mistook her for an angel.

'The wounds are not too deep and I can't see any thorns or dirt in them.'

She opened the tube of antiseptic cream and squeezed some on to her fingers.

'This will hurt a little.'

He closed his eyes again and felt her rub the cool cream gently into him. The pain did not matter. It would cleanse his wounds.

'There,' she said. 'Finished.'

He heard her begin to clear away the debris. He opened his eyes and caught sight of his dark, diluted blood splashed upon the kitchen table. The old woman wiped it away with the cloth and took the bowl to the sink.

'Thank you,' he said.

'Oh, it was nothing,' she replied, as she poured the bloodstained water away. She ran the cold water from the tap so that no stain would remain in the sink.

'I'll make a fresh pot of tea, shall I? And we'll have that cake.'

She dried her hands and refilled the kettle.

'Can I help?'

'No, no, no! You just sit there. You've done your work.'

He watched her set up the tray.

'Did you used to be a nurse?' he asked and knew at once it was a foolish question.

'What made you ask that?'

He pointed to his head.

'Oh no,' she laughed. 'Any mother learns how to clean wounds.'

'I thought your son might have become a doctor because of you....'

'No. That was his father's idea. It was a dream they both shared.'

She stopped for a moment and looked out into the garden.

'His father had always wanted his son to go out into the world and heal the sick.'

She paused, as a shadow rushed across the garden.

'All I wanted was for my son to be happy and safe, here in the garden. But I knew he would have to leave. Go to school and university.'

The water began to boil.

'You must have been proud of him when he became a doctor.'

'You should have seen him when he was a child. So full of energy and the joy of life. He would play and play out there. Even when the sunlight filled the garden, his light would seem brighter still. Such bold, brilliant innocence.'

The water was boiling fiercely now, spattering from the spout onto the tiles and window.

'If only he could have stayed like that forever,' she sighed. 'As soon as he left, the world changed him. His innocence became blunted. I could feel it and see it in him, even in his schooldays. Bit by bit the world changed him. Such hurt. Such stupidity. Such indifference!'

The kettle clicked and she poured the boiling water into the pot.

'Listen to me,' she chuckled. 'Like some old fool!'
She placed the teapot onto the tray.
'Let me take that.'
'Thank you,' she said and led the way out to the garden.
They sat in the sunlight, eating cake, while the tea cooled, and the boy bathed in the wonder of it all.
'You do have a beautiful garden,' he said.
She smiled.
'My husband worked hard to create all this. It is all his work.'
'He must have been very proud of it.'
'We both loved it. This is my favourite place to be. When my husband died I spread his ashes over the garden and, when I die, my son will do the same for me.'
She took a sip of tea from her cup.
'You look shocked? Of course, you are too young to be thinking of such things! I should not have said anything. Forgive me. When I was your age, I didn't think of death at all either. You must think it strange that I would do such a thing. But we wanted to be together in a place we both loved. Where else could that be but our garden? I am close to him every day and, when I die, I will be closer still.'
The tea had cooled and they both drank to quench their thirst.
'Does your son come back to visit you?' he asked.
'Oh, yes. He returns every year. But he changes so much; sometimes I can hardly recognise him. When he first arrives, he is like a lost soul. He wanders the garden and lies in his shelter. I can see the pain in his eyes. All the suffering he has to deal with eats into his

soul. We sit here and, eventually he begins to talk about his work. He has seen such brutality, such suffering.'

'Is that the cause of his pain?'

'No. His father had told him about the things he would see when he went out into the world.'

'Then what was it that caused him such pain?'

'After working out there for so many years, he found that he was becoming indifferent to it all. I think the task he had been faced with was so great; he was beginning to lose faith in himself. I remember, one evening, he said to me, "You know, mother, I am beginning to think that there is no hope for them after all. They do not deserve forgiveness because they know exactly what they do." But, despite all his despair, he knew he had to go back.'

She began to clear the cups and plates.

'I'll carry the tray,' he said.

'That's very kind of you,' she smiled.

'And I'll wash up.'

'There's no need.'

'I'd like to.'

'Very well,' she laughed. 'But I'll dry and put away.'

In the kitchen he ran the water and squeezed the liquid into the bowl.

'I'll put some of his music on,' she said and went into the sitting room.

He could feel the hot, soapy water begin to sting his hands. Now the old woman had left, the kitchen was filled with a silence he had not heard before. He stopped for a moment. The garden, filled with sunlight, seemed to be waiting for his return. Suddenly, out of the silence, a sound began. A simple musical phrase seemed to pierce his heart and, as it repeated itself, lifted his very soul to a world of dreams…

5

I was not there when my father died. His new partner telephoned and let me know. A heart attack, she said. He had been watching television and she had gone to make them a cup of tea. When she returned, he was dead. Sitting in the chair in front of the television.
After my mother's funeral he had been lost. He had hated being in the house on his own and had taken to drinking in his local club with his friends as company. He would telephone and say that he missed her terribly and did not know what to do. I would drive up to see him and we would go out to play golf. I would always meet him at the golf course. I could still not visit my mother's house. It was as though I was afraid of something. We would spend the best part of the day together and then I would leave. He would shake my hand and tell me to take care. His handshake had always seemed so strong. So full of life and the joy of being together. Now it seemed to be losing its warmth, its energy. And behind his false smile I could see the great emptiness that waited for him.
My mother had died in May. In November he met someone. In December he decided to sell the house and move in with her. She was good company he said. I could see that he was happier and tried to understand. It was difficult.
Just before Christmas we would have a family get together and my father brought her. How could I say no?
Needless to say the day did not go well. Polite

conversation did not last long and the atmosphere began to sour.

Eventually my father went out to his car and returned with some bags. At first we thought they contained presents, but they were filled with photographs. Family photographs. He did not want them anymore. My brothers were stunned and then very angry. He didn't need them, he said. He had his memories. And he pointed to his head. His grandchildren did not understand and began to cry. It was as though he was throwing them away. Could he not just keep them in a cupboard, perhaps? No. He had his memories.

Things were said and he left. My brothers would never speak to him again.

We sorted through the bags and shared out the photographs between us. I remember looking at them and thinking, how could he throw this away? I could never do that. When I hold a photograph of someone, there seems to be part of that person there with me. As though they have allowed themselves to be captured on film to remind us that the moment had been real and not a dream…

"God forgot me and I fell."

The dream of the son…

"…grant them rest, eternal rest."

Pie Jesu

1

She had wanted to go for a long time and he had promised to go with her. The morning of their visit had not started well. He had woken at some ungodly hour with a splitting headache and thought he might have to cancel the whole idea. Having taken the two pills, he lay with his head pressed against the pillows and listened to her snoring beside him. By the time the alarm rang, the pills had released him from his pain.
'Is it that time already?' she grumbled.
'I'll get up and make some tea,' he said, switching on the radio so that she could listen to her beloved radio four. He sat on the edge of the bed and let his fifty-six year old body come to terms with another day.
'Are you all right?' she asked.
'Yes, just waking up,' he yawned.
'Did you sleep all right?'
'I woke up a few times.'
'Dreaming again?'
'Yes,' he sighed. 'The same house and garden. I keep going there every time. I know we shouldn't be there, but something keeps us going back.'
'Was I with you again?'
'Yes, you're always there.'
'Did you find the broken room this time?'
'No, but I knew it was there. The roof would still be missing and the sky would be filled with stars. No, I went through the garden this time. I found a path that led past the greenhouse and down the side of a stream that flowed into a river at the bottom of the garden. There was a bank along the river and people were passing by. They were all laughing and talking. I tried

to talk to them but it was though they couldn't see me. I remember rushing back to the house to find you. I called and called. But you weren't there. I started to climb the red stairs to the room and a figure appeared at the top of the stairs. It didn't move or speak. It just stood there. I tried to call out but no soundcame…
Then, I woke up.'
'I'm glad I don't have dreams like that.'
'You said you never dream.'
'I must do…I just don't remember them.'
'Well, I haven't had dreams like these for years. Not since I was a boy.'
'I'll get a shower while you make the tea.'
He went downstairs, holding on to the banister, afraid he might fall again. It was that last step he had missed some years before. It had sent him crashing to the floor breaking an arm and tearing a tendon in his foot. Ever since then he had known how easy it was to break and had been afraid. Worse still, he was haunted by the fact that colleagues and friends the same age as him were dropping dead around him. He remembered the same thing had happened to his father and how his father had suddenly changed into an old man.
'Get past fifty five and your body can't do what it used to anymore,' he had warned and now he could feel it coming true.
He made the tea and took it up to the bedroom, switching on the main light so he could find her placemat and put the tea by her side of the bed. He turned on the side light on his side of the bed and went back to turn off the main light. Catching sight of the photograph of them taken some twenty years ago, he smiled. It was something that brought joy to his heart

every day. That someone so young, so beautiful and so clever had chosen him. He listened to her finishing in the shower and wondered about having two more pills with his tea but it would only make her worry and he didn't want to do that, knowing how much she was looking forward to returning to her old college. Besides the pain had gone and the hotel had been paid for. He tried his tea but it was still too hot and burnt the end of his tongue. She came in; the towel wrapped around her, and sat on the bed.

'Thanks, love.'

'Don't drink it yet. It's still too hot.'

She switched on the hair dryer and began to dry her hair. It was a routine he had always loved. She pushed her fingers through her hair and waggled the dryer to let the hot air blow through. As she did so, she would close her eyes and tip her head back in the soft light and he would bathe in her beauty and the warm air that flowed over him. By the time she had finished the tea had cooled enough for them to drink.

'I thought we would set off straight away and have breakfast at that little service station,' he suggested.

'Fine, love. I'll finish packing while you shower then.'

He showered and dried himself. Standing naked in front of the cold mirror, he shaved and then brushed his teeth. Teeth ground down by age and the nagging worries of everyday life. He closed the shower room window now that the condensation had gone and returned to the bedroom.

'I put a new toothbrush in your bag,' she said. 'I thought you might need one.'

'Okay…Should I pack some trousers for when we go down for dinner?'

'I would think so, love…Just in case.'
He dressed, packed the trousers and a shirt and took the cups downstairs to wash. She came downstairs with her overnight bag.
'Are you ready?'
'Just need to check everywhere's locked.'
'I'll do that…You go and get your bag and load the car.'
By the time she had checked the windows and the locks and gone to the toilet, he had loaded the car and was wiping the condensation from the windows.
'Have you got everything?' she asked, the front door key in her hand.
'Yes, I think so.'
'Do you need to go to the toilet?'
'I'm not a child!'
'I know that…So you don't need to go?'
'No, love.'
'Right,' she said and locked the door.
He sat in the driving seat and adjusted the mirror and she bustled into the seat beside him, sorting a place for her bag, a box of tissues, the road atlas and the mints for the journey. He always liked his mints to chew on the way. They helped him to concentrate.
'You know the way?' she asked.
'Yes…I marked it on the map.'
As he turned on the engine and she sorted the page in the atlas, he suddenly said, 'Did you put my jacket in?'
'No,' she sighed in exasperation.
'I'll need it in case it rains, won't I?'
'But I've locked up…'
He unfastened his seat belt.
'I asked you and you said…'

'Give me the keys…I'll get it.'
She searched through her handbag and handed him the keys.
'Keep your hair on,' he teased. 'It's not the end of the world. We've got plenty of time.'

The journey to Norwich would take them over three hours and so they stopped at a small service station on the A14 for a break. He parked the car and crawled out of the driver's seat. Age had taken its toll on his back and he stretched to ease the dull ache. Driving into the autumn sunshine had not helped the pain in his head and he knew he would have to take more pills. Once inside, they found a place in the non-smoking section and he felt the twinge in his back again, as he sat down.
'I think I'll have the full breakfast,' he said, studying her face to catch her reaction.
She looked at him and he knew he would change his mind.
'I'll have a croissant and coffee,' she muttered.
'They do Earl Grey,' he suggested.
'No, coffee will be fine.'
A boy, with his scribble pad, came to the table.
'Are you ready to order, sir?'
He looked at his wife, knowing the boy had done the wrong thing to ask him first.
'I would like a croissant and coffee, please!' she growled. 'Black with no sugar.'
The boy jotted down the order and turned to him.
'Erm…'
He was trying to make it look as though he was trying to come to some decision.

'I'll have the breakfast bap, please,' he grinned. 'And an Earl Grey.'

'What would you like in the bap, sir?'

He studied the menu. The choice was three from four. Difficult. As she tapped her fingers on the table and the boy held his small pen over his greasy pad, he knew he was taking too long.

'Er…'

He scratched the back of his neck. It shouldn't be this difficult.

'I'll have the egg, bacon and sausage, I think,' he said, pushing the plastic menu back into its place.

The boy took the order to the food counter, spoke to the chef and returned.

'Sorry, sir, we have no Earl Grey.'

'Just tea then,' he smiled.

'Are you sure you'll want to drink it?' she asked, as the boy shuffled back to the chef.

'It'll be all right. What do you want to do when we get there?' he asked, in the hope she would start talking.

'Find the hotel and check in, I suppose.'

'I know…but after that. Where do you want to go?'

'I thought the main thing was to find my old college…See if it's still there.'

'Do you want to go there first or look round the town…I thought we could look round the town and…'

'Yes, okay…I'm not sure how much it will have changed…I probably won't recognise the place.'

'But if we do that first, while the weather's so good, we could get some lunch, go back to the hotel and then drive round to look for places…You went to school there, didn't you?'

'Yes, but that was ages ago…I don't think I could find it now.'

The boy brought the drinks and the croissant.

'Your breakfast bap is just coming, sir' he smiled and left them.

'I need to visit the toilet,' she said and eased her way out from behind the table.

As she found her way to the toilet area, he fumbled through his pocket and found some pills. He popped them out of the sealed wrapper and poured himself a cup of dark brown tea. He added two small cartons of the long life milk and took one of the pills. He tried to swallow but could feel it sticking in his throat. He sipped the tea and swallowed again. It burnt his tongue and back of his mouth. The second pill seemed to slide down more easily, but he still had to swallow some of the hot tea to stop it lodging in his throat. The boy carried his breakfast bap to the table.

'Thank you,' he grimaced and bit into the soft bread, hoping it would ease the burning tip of his tongue.

'Everything all right, sir?' the boy asked, noticing the wrapper for the pills on the table and concerned that his customer might have a complaint.

'Yes, fine,' he said. 'I just burnt my tongue.'

'The tea was hot, sir,' the boy explained, fearing the customer might not have realised and that he should have said something.

'I know…I know…it was my fault…Drank it too quickly.'

He could see the relief on the boy's face and took another bite from the bap to reassure him.

'Take care the breakfast bap is not too hot, sir,' the boy warned, to cover himself.

'Yes, I will,' he nodded and noticed she was returning. 'Ah, here she is,' he said, as though his wife's return would solve everything. As the boy left, he noticed the pill wrapper and put it into his pocket.
'Everything all right?' he asked.
'No,' she grunted. 'There was a terrorist in there who wanted to take me hostage. Of course it was all right!'
He took another bite and the yolk from the egg exploded from the bottom of the bap over the table-top.
'Bugger!' he said and small particles of dry bread shot from his mouth.
'I knew you shouldn't have had it,' she grinned. 'You know greasy food is bad for you.'
While she nibbled at her croissant, he finished the bap. The grease coated his tongue and the food lay in his stomach. The tea was still too hot to drink.
'I think I'll go to the toilet before we go,' he said, as he slid out from behind the table.
'Look out for the terrorists!' she called after him.
He pushed through the swing door, entered the small passageway and found the door to the gents. Once inside, he found the pack of mints in his pocket and took one to get rid of the taste in his mouth. He unzipped his trousers and stood by a urinal and waited. He hated these public places. No matter how much they were cleaned, they always carried the sweet odour of urine and stale farts. If he didn't start urinating soon and someone came in, he knew he would have to pretend he had finished and leave. That would mean holding on until they reached the hotel, or making an excuse for another stop on the way. He waited and waited and then felt the first trickle, which turned into

a flow, much to his relief. He finished, washed and dried his hands.

The door was pushed open and the usual stranger came in. They nodded to each other. The man didn't look like a terrorist. He was holding the door open for him and terrorists didn't do that.

'Thank you,' he said and managed to stop himself adding, 'Have a good day.'

The toilet door hissed and grunted as it closed behind him. He made his way back to the table and could see that she was struggling with her coffee. He crunched the mint into small pieces and felt them rub against the sore tip of his tongue.

'That terrorist is still in there,' he joked, as he sat down. 'But I sorted him out...Used my SAS training. He won't bother you again.'

'Thanks for taking me today,' she said suddenly.

'That's all right, love. It's something you've always said you wanted to do.'

'I know,' she said. 'But it's a long way...Are you going to be okay to drive?'

'Yes...You can sit back and sleep on the way if you want.'

'I'll drive some of the way...'

'No...Leave it to me. You know you hate driving.'

He smiled at her and felt the nagging pain at the back of his eye.

'Are you sure?'

'It was my idea, wasn't it?'

She smiled at him.

'You are funny,' she said.

'Not according to that terrorist in the toilet,' he said.

By the time he had finished the mint, the tea had

cooled. He drank some and immediately regretted it. He could see that she was waiting.
'Are you not having your coffee?' he asked.
'No...it was horrible.'
'Let's go then.'
They paid the bill and left.

It took another two hours to reach the hotel. They parked the car on the gravel drive and checked in. The receptionist apologised but their room had not been cleaned yet as the room was not available until two o'clock. They had two hours to kill. They threw their bags into the back of the car and decided to walk into the centre of Norwich. The sun was shining and the day was warm, almost like spring. They crossed the road and strolled through a small park.
'Where do you want to go?' he asked.
'Let me get my bearings,' she said. 'I haven't been here for over twenty years. It's bound to have changed.'
They found some signs for the market and walked around the back of a library. He could see the disappointment on her face as they followed the steps down.
'This used to be such a colourful place,' she said. 'Great canopies over the stalls. Now look at it...'
Each stall seemed to be contained in a metal box that could be opened each day and secured at night. The stallholders stood drinking from plastic cups or sat on stools reading the day's paper, while people drifted by.
'Do you want to look round?'
'No,' she sighed and held his hand. 'Come on...If we go down here we come to the old part of the town.'
They left the crowds and the paving gave way to

narrow, cobbled streets. She had hoped that there might be some interesting shops, but the buildings seemed to have been abandoned. The autumn sun was too low in the sky for its light and warmth to fall on the narrow streets and people hurried through to reach the main shopping areas. Eventually, they reached a main road again and a lorry roared past and shook the air around them.

'I know where we are now!' she announced. 'This is the main bus route...Just up here is the cathedral!'

They climbed the hill and there, in its great space, behind its old wall, bathed in the golden light was the cathedral.

'Do you want to go in?' he asked, hoping she would rather look for a place to eat.

'We could look round,' she said.

He felt uncomfortable standing in the vast emptiness of the cathedral. Its great height did not raise him up, but made him feel small. There seemed to be no warmth in the building. The hard stone gave no comfort to a lost soul. Dust from the decaying walls seemed to hang in the air and made him cough. Except for the few tourists, the place was empty of life. They wandered aimlessly amongst the images of Christ and the great myth that was supposed to provide salvation for the soul in this life and the next. They passed the tombs of bishops and people deemed worthy enough to be buried in such a place and he knew he needed to be outside. This place expected too much of anyone and gave nothing in return except a promised dream and he did not believe in that dream any more, not since his parents had been taken from him. His soul needed the comfort of human touch, most of all, his wife. He needed the touch of her body next to his more than anything. He could see she was studying something on the floor. He crossed to her and put his arm around her waist.

'Hello...who could this be?' she laughed and turned to him.

'Who did you expect?' he asked.

'Does this mean you've had enough and want to go?'

She slipped her arm around his waist.

'Only if you are ready...I thought we might get coffee and cake somewhere.'

'That sounds like a good idea...I was just looking at this.'

She pointed to the gravestone in the floor.

'IN SACRED MEMORY' was inscribed at the top.

They left the cathedral grounds and followed the road past the old castle.

'It was here that we caught the bus home,' she explained. 'And there should be a pub along here, where I'd go for a drink with dad.'

'What? Even when you were sixteen?'

'Yes...it was funny. They'd let me in but would question how old my sister was, even though she was nineteen...It would make dad laugh.'

'And he would let you drink?'

'Only a half. It used to be a Saturday ritual...shopping on the market...the pub for a drink and the bus home. Dad would go up to bed and have his afternoon siesta while we helped mum.'

No matter how much they searched, it could not be found.

'Never mind, love,' he consoled her.
'I was really looking forward to that…Just to sit where we used to sit.'
He knew how much her father had meant to her. When he was alive they had phoned each other every day. She would share her bad days at work with him and he would tell her not to let the bastards grind her down. No matter what the problem he could always talk her through it. She would always feel better after their time together. His death had hurt her deeply. Although he had recovered from a heart attack and a broken hip, his diabetes had worn him down. His eyesight had faded so that he could not do his beloved crossword and the sores on his legs never seem to heal. Having caught the dreaded MRSA in hospital, he had been trapped in an isolation room and given up. He did not want to live anymore. His body was of no more use to him. Her great regret was that she had not been there. They had been on holiday and she had not spoken to him for several days. Although the years had passed, she had not really recovered. Brief chats on the phone to her mother were not the same and, even though he talked with her about work, it was not the same. It could never be the same. Her father, whom she loved more than anyone, had been taken from her or, worse still, had chosen to leave.
As they wandered through the crowded streets they realised they were heading back to the markets. They stopped to consider taking another direction and noticed to their left at the top of a hill a large glass-fronted building.
'Have you not been to our wonderful centre?' an old man asked. 'It's well worth a visit…'

The old man smiled at them and could tell that they were confused.

'Don't tell me that a Scotsman has to tell an Englishman about his own town!' he joked.

'We don't live here,' he explained. 'We've just come across from Birmingham.'

'And why on earth would you want to visit Norwich?'

'I used to live here over twenty years ago,' she added.

'Twenty years ago! There's been a lot o' changes since then!'

'Yes…we're just trying to find our way round…We've been to the cathedral.'

'Which one? We've two, you know.'

'I know,' she said. 'There's the Catholic one as well.'

'I've never seen so many churches either,' he grinned.

'Ah, yes…we're full of those,' the old man nodded. 'But that building you see up there is well worth a visit.'

'We were looking for something to eat…a cake and a coffee.'

'Oh, you'll get that up there…There's like coffee shops and the like…And there's a place where you can get books. They let you have books. You don't have to pay for them but they do expect you to bring them back when you have finished them. And there's lots of charity shops and an information centre and if you go up the stairs there's a television centre and some local radio stations. The charity shops aren't cheap mind but they're for good causes. I've got to go up there in an hour. It's my turn on the cancer stall…My wife died of cancer about ten years ago…It keeps me busy, you know…And there's a place where you can get free books. It's downstairs. Just in front of you as you go in. And the coffee shop is on your right. And the charity shops are on the left. Have you got your Christmas cards yet? Plenty of cards to choose from in there.'

'How do you know all this?' he asked, enjoying the moment.

'I've lived here for over twenty years…Came down for the work…Raised our family here…My daughter's in Leeds…teaching…but she's going to pack up this year. It's getting too much…and my youngest is in banking. He works in London…Have you seen our new shopping centre?'

'No.'

'Oh, yes! Our latest development! It's supposed to be our hope for the future, but I don't think it will last. I watch them all go in, all excited about being somewhere new. Not many come out with bags mind. London prices. People can't afford it…Are you here for the day then?'

'Yes,' she said, warming to the old man's company. 'I used to go to college here.'

'My daughter went to college…in Leeds. She teaches there now. Not for much longer though. She doesn't like it anymore…She might come back…My son's in London. Something to do with banking…He phones me once in a while…I don't want to go down to London. It's too big…He's going to Hong Kong soon…Got a position out there for three years…An opportunity, he says…Going to take the family out there…Might see them this Boxing Day. An old man can dream dreams, you know.'

He could see that the old man was becoming lost in his own thoughts.

'Well, thanks for your help.'
'You're most welcome...It's just up there, look. If you go straight in the coffee shop is on the right.'
'Thank you. Good to have met you. Take care.'
As they climbed the hill, they turned and saw him talking to other strangers.
'Poor man,' she sighed. 'Did you hear how he kept repeating himself?'
'We all do that, love...I thought he was good...passing his time, helping people.'
The centre was just as the old man had described. They ordered their coffee and cake, found a table and sat to watch the world go by.
'I still miss him, you know,' she said, a tear forming in her eye.
'I know, love,' was all he could say.

When they returned to the hotel, their room was ready. He carried their overnight bags up the stairs and she let them in to the room.
'This is lovely,' she said. 'Much bigger than I expected...And look! That's our wallpaper! It's the same paper we have in our sitting room!'
He put the bags onto the queen-size bed, while she explored the ensuite bathroom.
'Plenty of room in here as well,' she called. 'The shower cubicle is almost as big as the ones we have on holiday in the States...Come and have a look.'
He joined her in the bathroom to admire the shower.
'Where do you want your clothes?'
'I'll come and unpack.'
'I thought we'd try and find your college this afternoon. So, if we unpack, we can go straight away.'

'Do you think we'll have time to find my old school as well?'
'We'll have to look on the map.'
'Well, you do that, while I unpack.'
He found the old Ordnance Survey map and sat on the bed to study it. She had found it at home and brought it with them. He set it against the road atlas.
'It looks easy enough,' he said. 'Just go back the way we came and the road forks to the left to go towards Ipswich. We have to go over a railway bridge and there should be a turning on the right. Then its follow the lanes to Keswick Hall.'
'I remember a turning into the lane leading to the college. You have to turn left I think. I always remember the coach having a terrible time trying to get round in the winter.'
'Yes, that would make sense on the map. There is a right turn and it leads to the hall.'
'There we are...Finished...That didn't take very long. All your things are in the bottom drawer...Now let me see.'
She came and sat on the bed and leaned against him.
'You'll have to use the atlas so far and the map when we are nearly there,' he explained. 'See...Here's the road we came in on and it forks just here.'
'Yes, daddy!' she teased.
'What did you say that for,' he grumbled.
'You were talking to me like I was a little girl.'
'Well, if you don't want me to show you...' he said and pushed her playfully away.
She laughed and snuggled up to him again.
'I was only teasing, grumpy bear! Come on. Show me. I'm looking.'

'Can you see how the two match up? That's the Ipswich road and we should turn off there.'

'I see.'

'It might have changed a lot because this is an old map, but the main road wouldn't be that different and, if we look out for the railway bridge, we should be all right.'

'Okay, I'll just go to the toilet and then we can go.'

He folded the map so that she could see the section they needed and marked the page in the road atlas. As he stood, he felt pain returning and knew he would need more pills. He took them out of his coat pocket and waited for her to come out. The toilet flushed and he could hear her washing her hands. Eventually she bustled out of the bathroom.

'Do you think we'll have time to go and see my old school?' she asked again. 'It was in Sprowston.'

'I should think so…I need to go to the toilet as well,' he said and brushed past her. 'There's a small map of Norwich on the back of that leaflet by the side of the bed. It might be on there.'

He closed the door. There was a glass on the shelf above the sink. He rinsed it out and filled it with water. The pills were like stones in his mouth and the chilled water made his gums hurt. He swallowed hard and felt them stick in the back of his throat. He drank again and the pills scraped their way down. He leaned on the sink and pressed his forehead against the mirror. The pain would go. He knew it would go. It was just a matter of time. He had another drink and flushed the toilet.

'Ready to go, then?' he asked, as he opened the door and smiled brightly.

She was sitting on the bed, studying the back of the leaflet.

'We'll need to go round the ring road to get to Sprowston.'
'Okay, let's go then.'
She looked at his face.
'Are you sure you're going to be all right?'
'Yes, fine, love…Come on, I want to see where you spent your life before we met. You've always talked about it. All those things you got up to when you were a student.'
He grabbed his coat and took her by the hand.
'My lady, your coach awaits.'
'Do you think we'll need coats?'
'No…Probably not…But take them just in case.'
They locked the room and went down to the car. He could see the excitement of anticipation in her face and it eased his pain. The warm autumn sunshine cast long shadows behind them.

Finding the Ipswich road and following it to the turning for Keswick was not a problem, but they soon realised they had missed a turn they needed to take them to Keswick Hall and were lost.
'I don't recognise any of this,' she said. 'We'll have to turn and go back.'
He noticed an old lady walking her dog and slowed down.
'I'll ask her,' he said, pulled up beside her and wound down the window.
'Excuse me,' he called.
The old lady stopped and turned to them. She did not seem surprised to see them. It was almost as though she had been expecting them. Her hair was so thin he could see the sores on her scalp.

'Are you lost?' she asked.

The old dog stood panting and slobbering beside her, as though it was glad of the rest.

'Yes…I'm looking for Keswick Hall?'

'You've come too far,' she coughed and pointed back down the road. He noticed the torn sleeve and the soiled coat.

The dog sank to the ground and gave out a deep sigh.

'You need to turn round and go back about a mile and there's a turning on the left,' she explained. 'And then it's the next left. Not very far.'

Weeping sores covered the woman's bare legs.

'Thank you,' he smiled.

'You can turn round up there.'

The old woman pointed to a field entrance ahead of them.

'Thank you,' he smiled again, as he wound up the window.

He drove up to the entrance and reversed into it. As he checked the road was clear, he caught sight of the old woman trying to make the dog stand up. He watched her pull at the dog's collar. It was no use. The dog could not get up. She bent down and pushed her arms under the dog's neck and tail to try to raise it. The dog's head lolled against her coat sleeve, slobber seeping from its mouth. Its weight taken by the old woman, the dog kicked and scrambled to place its feet on the ground. Such a great struggle made the dog wretch and vomit onto the ground. Gently, the old woman released her grip and the dog stood, shaking in its effort to stay alive, unable to move. The old woman straightened herself and waited by the side of the old dog, which was beginning to eat its own vomit. As they

passed, the two figures seemed trapped in time, waiting for something to happen.
'Poor things,' he said.
'What?' she asked.
'The old woman and her dog.'
'What dog?'
'The old woman's dog.'
'I didn't see a dog,' she said and looked back.
He glanced in the rear view mirror. The road was empty.
'The old woman, with the sores on her, had a dog,' he tried to explain, checking his mirror again. 'Didn't you see her trying to lift it?'
'No…I didn't see a dog at all.'
'But I saw…'
'Here's the turning!' she warned.

They did not have to travel very far before she recognised where they were.
'It's here! It's here!' she called in her excitement. 'This is where the coach turned. Turn left down that lane…Look. I'm right. There's the sign.'
Although they drove slowly along the lane, he nearly missed the entrance. He braked sharply and pulled into the gravel drive. Ahead of them a large grey-white building shone in the sunlight.
'This is it!' she shouted. 'This is my old college.'
He followed the signs that led to the car park at the side of the building. There were no barriers and the car park was no more than a piece of barren ground in the midst of ancient trees, divided into sections by old railway sleepers. He found a space under an old acer, which seemed to be burning in the autumn light. He

switched off the engine and unfastened his seat belt.

'What are we going to do?' she asked.

'Have a look round.'

'Are you sure we can?'

'Of course…we haven't come all this way to sit in the car.'

'What if someone stops us?'

'We'll tell them we have come to look round because you used to live here and we're thinking of buying the place.'

'Don't be stupid!'

'Come on…Nobody's going to be interested in a couple of old people like us.'

'Who are you calling old?' she joked, unbuckling her belt.

They were about to get out when they both saw the butterfly drop out of the sunlight onto the windscreen. It settled itself and spread its wings.

'Where on earth did that come from?' he whispered.

'There shouldn't be any butterflies out at this time of year, should there?'

They sat, transfixed by this moment of delicate beauty. A butterfly, in the dying light of autumn, had found them. Suddenly it flitted from the windscreen and seemed to dance before them, spiralling up into the beam of sunlight. They leaned forward trying to follow it but a cloud's shadow passed over them and the butterfly had disappeared.

When they got out of the car, she held onto his arm and they followed a path through the trees. It led out onto a grassed area by the side of the building and she knew instantly where they were.

'We would sit out here in the summer and revise for exams,' she announced. 'And I'm sure that's my old room!'

This section of the building had been converted into apartments. She let go of his arm and rushed across the grass.

'It was here! It was here!'

She was almost dancing in front of some windows. When he reached her, he could see that the apartment was empty and presumed the people were out for the day.

'There didn't used to be a kitchen there,' she explained. 'It looks like they've taken the two bedrooms this side and changed them into a kitchen and sitting room. But this one…this one used to be my room! The others would knock on my window if they were late back and climb in…Let's go round the back!'

In her enthusiasm, all thought of trespass had disappeared. It was as though she had suddenly become the young, carefree woman he had fallen in love with long ago. Caught up in her excitement for life and disregard for any bureaucratic rules, he had followed her then as he followed her now. For that moment the great weight of responsibility had been lifted from them, as they raced each other to the rear of the building. A wide gravel path with a low wall that separated it from a large field was set back from the whole length of the building. The college had been divided into apartments, offices, small businesses and conference rooms. As they followed the path, she pointed out where she had attended lectures and seminars. So many memories came flitting back, like little butterflies dancing around her in the sunlight, and

he bathed in the brightness that seemed to surround her. Suddenly she let go of him again.
'I think the dining room was behind that hedge!' she said. 'Let's go and see!'
'No. I'll wait here,' he said and sat on the wall.
She raced across the grass and through a gap in the hedge. He looked around. He was alone. Now she was gone, there seemed to be nothing to see. He could hear the distant roar of traffic. The wall felt cold beneath him. It was getting late in the afternoon. He knew the sun would be setting soon and be replaced by the dark chill of night. He got down from the wall and put his hands in his pockets. Perhaps they should have worn their coats. She returned, a little disappointed.
'I couldn't see in,' she said, linking her arm into his.
He felt complete again, as he always did when they walked like this.
'Never mind, love. Is there anywhere else you want to find?'
'The union's house used to be over there. I was vice-president for a year. I'd like to see that if we could.'
They crossed some grass and followed a walkway between some apartments but could not find the union building.
'It must have been further down,' she sighed.
'Do you want to go on?'
'No, let's turn round and go back. I've seen enough.'
'If you're sure...'
They returned to the rear of the college. As they approached the gravel path, she let go of his arm and ran on ahead. She climbed onto the low wall that separated field from path and raised her arms like wings.

'What are you doing?'
'Come on!' she called. 'Follow me!'
She began to walk along the wall.
'Wait a minute!' he called. 'We can't…'
She stopped and turned to him, a fierce, determined look on her face.
'Are you telling me that you are afraid to follow me?'
'No, it's just…'
'It's perfectly safe. We won't fall.'
'I know that…'
'Well, come on then!'
'What if…?'
'I'll come back and help you.'
She walked back and held out her hand.
'It's all right I can do it.'
He clambered onto the end of the wall and they stood facing each other.
'There you are,' she said. 'I told you.'
Suddenly she turned, spread her arms and began to run along the wall.
'Come on!' she called 'It's easy.'
He looked down at the wet, slimed surface. The roar of traffic on a distant motorway began to fill the air.

The lorry was coming. He knew the lorry was coming. He could feel the earth trembling beneath the wall.

When he was young, he was not afraid of falling. But now! He raised his arms, took a deep breath and began to walk.
She was already half way.
'Slow down!' he shouted. 'Wait for me!'

She stopped and turned. He could see her great, radiant smile and her arms open wide, waiting to embrace him.

'Come on!' she shouted. 'You've got to run…Run, love, run!'

He could feel himself beginning to panic and fought to stay on the wall. Summoning all his courage and concentration, he began to walk more quickly. Suddenly she turned and raced away.

'Don't leave me here!' he shouted and began to run.

She leapt from the end of the wall, arms outstretched as though she was about to fly. He thought for a moment that she was going to disappear and felt a great urge to cry out. She landed safely and turned to wait for him. Watching her, he lost all fear of falling and ran as fast as he could. He jumped down from the wall and landed awkwardly beside her.

'You're crazy!' he gasped. 'I thought I was going to lose you.'

'What made you say that?'

'I don't know.'

'You know I'd never leave you.'

She reached the end of the wall and took a great leap into the air, arms outstretched like wings. He thought for a moment that she was going to disappear and felt a great urge to cry out. She landed safely and turned to wait for him. He jumped down from the wall and landed clumsily beside her.

'I thought I was going to lose you!' he gasped.

'What made you think that? You know that will never happen. I'll always be with you.'

They hugged each other tightly and kissed for the first time that day. They put their arms around each other and returned to the car park. He felt safe again. He unlocked the car.
'Thank you for this,' she said. 'I will remember it forever.'
'Even without the photos?'
'Even without the photos!' she smiled.
As she got into her car seat she noticed a leaf from the acer tree had stuck to her shoe. She held it between her fingers and was about to throw it away.
'No,' he said. 'Let's keep it. It will help us to remember.'

'You're crazy!' he gasped. 'I thought I was going to lose you.'
'What made you say that?'
'I don't know.'
'You know I'd never leave you.'
They hugged each other and walked back to the car. As she got in and sat down, she noticed a small leaf from the acer tree had stuck to her shoe. She opened the door to throw it away.
'No!' he said. 'Don't throw it away…Keep it as a memory.'

"...because you are merciful."

Agnus Dei

3

He woke. His heart was pounding. It was difficult to breathe. He felt the plastic oxygen mask pressed against his mouth. He reached to pull it away and felt the plastic tube pull against his arm. He opened his eyes and saw the familiar surroundings. Metal bed. Drips. Sink. Small cupboard. A jug of dead water. Bare walls.

He could hear the same old man calling out in despair, 'Can I get up now? Nurse! Can I get up now?'

He could feel the cold sweat clinging to him. He lay back on his pillow and began to breathe more slowly. She had gone. He was alone.

He lay for a while and let the tears flow, as he tried to remember the dream. But it was gone. Carefully, he reached across for the box of tissues on the bedside cabinet. He pulled one out and dabbed away the tears. He noticed the book by the side of the box, switched on the bedside light, put on his glasses and reached for it. It was a small book of poetry. They had bought it for each other on their visit to Norwich some years ago. He opened it and a small blood-red leaf of an Acer fell onto his white sheet. He picked it up and felt its stiff fragility between his thumb and finger. Gently, he placed it back into the front of the book. On its title page he had written 'To each other, a sacred memory.'

I was not there when my father died. His new partner telephoned and let me know. A heart attack, she said. He had been watching television and she had gone to make them a cup of tea.

When she returned, he was dead. Sitting in the chair in front of the television.
After my mother's funeral he had been lost. He had hated being in the house on his own and had taken to drinking in his local club with his friends as company. He would telephone and say that he missed her terribly and did not know what to do. I would drive up to see him and we would go out to play golf. I would always meet him at the golf course. I could still not visit my mother's house. It was as though I was afraid of something. We would spend the best part of the day together and then I would leave. He would shake my hand and tell me to take care. His handshake had always seemed so strong. So full of life. Now it seemed to be losing its warmth, its energy. And, behind his false smile, I could see the great emptiness that waited for him.

He woke.
There was no book of poetry on the cabinet by the bed. No Acer leaf pressed between the pages, only plastic tubes, wounds that would not heal and a bag of piss.

He was standing at the foot of the bed waiting for him.
'I'm sorry,' he said. 'I must have fallen asleep.'
He shifted his weight so that the tube did not pull against his flesh.
'It's the morphine for the pain…Have you been here long?'
'No.'

'I'm dying, you know.'
'Yes.'
'I didn't think it would be like this. I thought God would strike me down before I killed them. I begged Him to. But He didn't. I warned Him but He wasn't listening. I said, 'Look at me, God. Look at what I am doing.' But He wasn't watching. I did it three times. You'd think He would have known. Even if He wasn't watching He would have found out about it. It was in all the papers. On the news. He must have known what I had done. Surely He would have…He should have stopped me. I wanted Him to.'
'The nurse said you wanted to talk to me.'
He shifted his weight again before answering.
'My mother liked you, you know. Such a nice boy she would say. Always polite. I think she wanted me to be like you…She's dead now, of course. Both my parents are dead. Gone to heaven to be with God. With the Father. God took them before they got old because he needed them more than me…Are your parents still alive?'
'No.'
'Have they gone to heaven?'
'I suppose so.'
'You don't sound sure.'
'No, I'm not sure.'
'Were they good people?'
'Yes…'
'Then they would go to heaven, wouldn't they?'
'Yes.'
'Don't you believe in heaven?'
'I'm not sure.'
'My parents went to heaven. God wanted them. He

125

took them. He didn't ask me. God doesn't have to ask, does He? If God wants you, He just takes you away to heaven to be with Him because He loves you so much…Did you cry when they died?'
'Yes…'
'So did I…People told me not to cry because they were safe now. Safe with God. In heaven…But I cried. I didn't want them to go to heaven. I wanted them to stay with me…Do you miss your parents?'
'Yes.'
'I miss mine…They were killed…An accident. Trying to miss a dog that had wandered into the road…Right at the beginning of their holiday…Perhaps God was not watching again.'
He laughed. A dry, dead laugh.
'The nurse said you wanted to ask me something.'
'Yes, we'll get to that.'
He winced as he shifted his weight again.
'Are you married?'
'Yes.'
'I was married…Do you love you wife?'
'Yes.'
'I loved my wife. More than anything…She helped me when my parents were killed. She told me they would be safe in heaven, no more suffering. She said…She explained that our lives are in God's hands and He has a purpose for our lives, but only He knows the purpose for our lives. We don't know the purpose, only He does. And we have to trust Him. We have to have faith in His mysterious ways. His mysterious ways…She always had faith in His mysterious ways. She would read from her bible to me, like my mother used to, and explain how we are loved by God and His

son because we are Christians and we live a good life…Do you read the bible?'
'No.'
'You don't know about God and Jesus?'
'Yes, I know about them.'
'God is the Father! Jesus is the son! And Mary is the holy Mother!'
'Yes, I know.'
'And Jesus was born in a stable…'
'I know.'
'I liked that story of the baby Jesus and the stable and the three wise men following the star. I used to read it. My mother would read it to me at Christmas…Such a good story.'
'Yes.'
'I had to go across to see them. Identify their bodies. They were in thick black bags in a cold room. I'd never seen them dead before. Some people say that dying is like going to sleep forever. They didn't look like they were asleep. I'd seen them asleep when I used to go into their bedroom with my nightmares. They didn't look like that. I would shout and cry and mother would wake up, startled from her sleep. She would wake up so quickly. One moment she would be asleep and then, in a flash, she would be awake. She would be there with me. With her soft, warm arms around me. And I would be safe again…but not then. Not when she was dead. I cried out but she would not come back. She had gone. They had both gone…'
'I know. I'm sorry…'
'My wife was killed in a car as well, crushed by a lorry on the motorway. It's funny that, isn't it? My parents and my wife taken the same way like that…The driver

had fallen asleep at the wheel and the lorry just drifted across. There was nothing she could have done. It just drifted across…Just…There seems to be so much in life that just happens! It just happens…They cut her out of the wreckage and took her to hospital and she lived for two days. And on the third day, she died. On the third! That's like Jesus; only different…I was with her when she died. I held her hand and cried. I prayed and prayed that she would wake up. God would save her. But she didn't wake up. She had gone before me and I was afraid. Not for her. For me.'

Blood began to seep into the bag of urine.

'You see I realised that deep down, deep in that secret place within myself, was an emptiness that would devour me and that emptiness had only been filled by the warmth of her body against mine. And He had taken her, the same as He had taken my parents before they could grow old…'

'I…' He tried to think of something to say but it was too late.

'Herod killed the children, you know…in the bible… when Jesus was born…He sent his soldiers to kill the newborn…At the same time the son of God came into the world, He allowed Herod to kill innocent children. Just think of that! Everything He had said about children and He allowed it to happen…He could have stopped it, of course he could. He is God! He can do anything…'

'What do you want me to do?'

'He should have stopped me!'

'I know…What do you want me to do?'

'There is a place where I spread their ashes. A safe place. I want you to take mine to them…Could you do

that? If I told you where it was, could you take me to them?'
'Yes…'
'Thank you…'
'Is there something else?'
'Yes. There was a secret. God had a secret and I need to tell you what it was…'

"It is finished."

The dream of
the Holy Spirit…

"I feel the trial and
wrath to come."

Libera me.

1

When they returned, they were afraid. Afraid it would not be the same. Afraid he would not remember them. They climbed the red stairway and pushed back the curtain. Casa had not changed at all, but they were surprised to find people already eating. It was late evening and the sun was already setting behind the Monchique mountains. They could see he was busy with some people and waited by the curtain. Perhaps they should have booked! He turned and noticed them. He smiled and came over to them.
'Welcome back, sir,' he said as they shook hands. 'Madame.'
'You remember us?' she asked, flattered by his welcome.
'Of course.'
'We didn't book, I'm afraid.'
'That is not a problem, Madame…If you would like to take a place on the balcony; I will come through to you in a moment. What can I get you to drink?'
'I'd like a gin and tonic.'
'And it is a tutti frutti for you, sir.'
'How did you remember that?' she gasped.
'I will not be long,' he smiled.
They walked out onto the balcony and sat at a table. People were there, finishing their drinks before being called through to their tables and they made polite conversation about the weather and their journeys. They were relieved when the waitress arrived and invited the others through to their tables. The owner came through with their drinks and placed them on the table.

'And how are you, sir?' he beamed.
'I'm fine,' he said and knew he had lied. He was not fine. He was tired, exhausted. Shortly after Christmas his father had been diagnosed with terminal cancer and been given only a few months to live. The pressure of work had meant he could only visit his father at weekends. It had started well, with plans to watch cricket together and to visit places they had been when his mother had been alive, but the cancer had taken hold and was aggressive, causing his body to shrivel and collapse in agonising pain, only subdued by increasing levels of morphine. And so the cricket and the journeys never happened. Eventually, his death was a release, a sudden heart attack, a different form of blessing. He had lasted four months, almost as long as the killings.
'And Madame?'
'Oh, we're fine,' she said. 'We are both retired now.'
'That is good to hear.'
'And how are you?'
The owner shrugged.
'We are much the same, Madame. Nothing changes. Each day is the same.'
'I see they are building the new apartments next to you,' she said.
'Yes. They are still not completed, Madame. Some dispute between the builder and the owner.'
A sudden howl came from below and echoed between the new building and the walls of the Casa.
'What on earth was that?' she gasped.
'It is my neighbour's dog, Madame. It is left alone at night. They must go out to work. It sits in the yard and waits for the night sky. I have watched it, Madame. As

the darkness comes and fills the yard it paces back and forth, pressed against the wall. And, when the sun has gone, it sits and gazes at the stars. It sits and gazes all night until its owners return.'
'How sad.'
'It is how they have chosen to lead their lives, Madame.'
'You are very busy tonight.'
'Yes, Madame.'
'The last time we were here there was just us.'
'I remember, Madame.'
'We were looking forward to talking with you but if you are busy…'
'Of course we can still talk. Perhaps later, Madame…Now I will leave you with the menu. There are your favourites, of course, but we also have some very fine lamb tonight. I think you would enjoy it, sir.'
'Thank you…I see you have a new waitress.'
'Yes, sir. She will come and take your order shortly.'
It did not take them very long to decide. She chose her favourite chicken and he wanted the lamb. When they returned inside, they were surprised and delighted to be seated at their usual table. The owner helped to serve at each table and talked to his guests as though they were friends he had known for many years. As they ate their meals in the subdued light, their favourite classical music played in the background.
'This is wonderful again,' she said. 'How's your lamb?'
'It is the best I've ever eaten.'
'Are you feeling all right?'
'Just tired, love.'

When the waitress had cleared their desserts, the owner brought them a coffee. By now they had the restaurant to themselves.

'Coffee, sir,' he smiled and left them for a moment.

He returned with a bottle and two small glasses.

'I thought you would like a small nightcap.'

'It's the special wine we had last time,' she laughed.

He joined them at their table and they talked; first of all about the mundane things that filled their lives and about the state of the world. Eventually, they began to talk about his early retirement. He explained about his father's death.

'And you were working on the murders of the three children at the same time, weren't you, love,' his wife added.

'Yes.'

'Did you hear about them over here?' she asked.

'Yes, Madame. I remember… It was in the newspapers.'

'It was terrible,' she continued. 'Terrible.'

'It was you, who caught him, sir?'

'He came to my station and gave himself up…'

'He asked for you, didn't he, love.'

'Yes.'

'Why was that?'

'I think he must have seen my name in the papers.'

'You suffered some terrible nightmares, didn't you, love?'

'Yes.'

'I'm sorry,' she said suddenly. 'I must use your toilet.'

'Yes, Madame. It is downstairs.'

His wife got up from the table and left them.

He sat for a moment in silence and turned the stem of

the glass in his fingers.
'It is good to see you again,' he said.
'And you, sir.'
And then he began.
'Every night it would be the same dream, the same nightmare. I would be in the garden. Not my garden. The one in my dream. It would be evening. Patches of sunlight. Long shadows. I would walk down the path. Pass flowers. Such a strong scent. Pass a greenhouse. Huge. Filled with seedlings. There would be a man in there, watering them. I don't know who he was. He had his back to me. I would call but he would not turn round. I'd walk further down the path. Pass a small orchard and a broken wall. There would be a lizard on the wall. It would dart into one of the holes as my shadow passed over it. The path leads down to a river. I could hear it behind the wall. And I start to search for the gate. It's broken and hangs crooked in its space. I have to lift it and push it open. I push hard but there's something on the other side blocking it. I push hard again and get my head and shoulders between the wall and gate. I can see the black plastic bag on the ground. The gate has jammed up against it. I reach down as far as I can and feel myself held between the rough edge of the gate and wall. I touch the bag. My fingers fumble against it, trying to take hold. It feels warm, as though its blackness has absorbed the heat from the last rays of sunlight. At last I take hold and pull. The plastic tears and sticks to my fingers. And then something dark flows out of the hole I have made and floats up to my mouth. It begins to fill my mouth and cover my face. I tear at it with my hand but the plastic on my fingers softens and runs into my eyes.'

'Why did he take the eyes?'
'How did you know about that?'
'Did he tell you?'
'He said he was afraid of them.'
'Why?'
'He had seen himself in their eyes. He thought part of him might be trapped in them. He thought, when the bodies were discovered, we might find an image of him in their eyes.'
'Like a photograph?'
'Yes.'
'Why did he do such things?'
'Why do any of us do such things? He said that it was to test God. Oh, don't misunderstand. He believed in Him. He believed all he had been told about a loving Father. An all-powerful being. Good and evil. Angels and heaven. He believed all that.'
'Then how could he do such a thing?'
'He believed God had taken his parents before their time. They were killed in a car crash over here. It had been a holiday they had planned for each other. They were going to return to a place they had been when he was a young boy. A special place full of memories… And then God took his wife in another crash and, when she was dying in hospital, they discovered she was pregnant. They hadn't known. She would have been forty, much younger than him. They had been trying for a long time and had given up hope. The child would have been their first and all they had dreamed of. A small miracle. And God had just taken it all from him again. It was that that turned his simple mind. It was clear to him that God was not a loving father but cruel, heartless. He searched through the bible.

God's acts of inhumanity seemed remorseless. He began to realise that Judas was not the villain but the victim of God's ordained plan. God had allowed his only son to suffer. He had turned his back on him, forsaken him.'

'Doesn't the crucifixion tell us that God shares in our suffering?'

'Jesus suffered. God watched.'

'But didn't God share in the suffering, like any parent would?'

'He had thought that for a long time, but then he asked himself the question. 'If it was in the parent's power to prevent or stop the pain, what would a loving parent do?' And the answer only confirmed God's indifference.'

'How could this justify what he did? Such a cruel act of futility.'

'It didn't. Nothing could. It was just that his simple mind had cracked. His inner rage became obsessed with God's apparent heartlessness and one night he came across the nativity again, searching for some hope, and found Herod's killing of the innocent children. Why hadn't God stopped it? Why had He allowed such a thing to happen at such a time? Could it be that God was not all-powerful? Were there some things He could not stop happening? In his great confusion, he decided to test God. He would become like Herod and take the lives of innocent children. He prayed to God to stop him, to strike him dead. When he took the first child, he wept. He raged at the second, cursing God's indifference to such a cruel act. And, with the third, he was struck with the horrific thought that, perhaps, God did not exist at all and that

everything he had done was for nothing. It was then he came to the station.'
'And he asked for you?'
'Yes…I had known him when he was a boy and I was a youth. He had remembered me. I had mended his heaven-stick and he thought I could do something for him.'
'What on earth was a heaven-stick?'
'He was a simple child and thought he could use a stick his father had given him to reach up to the stars and touch heaven…'
'And could you help him?'
'No…'
'But he had stopped.'
'Yes.'
'Perhaps God intervened at that point?'
'And allowed the deaths of three innocent children?'
'I cannot explain such a thing…It is beyond our understanding!'
'Yes, I thought you might say that! It's funny, isn't it? Whenever we can't explain God's action or inaction, we fall back on that. Beyond our understanding!'
In the silence between them, they heard his wife climbing the stairway.
'I met your daughter downstairs and she tells me you are going to make some changes,' she announced, as she pushed back the curtain.
'Yes, Madame. She thinks we should make the downstairs into a seating area and have a bar. When they first come, people are a little confused because downstairs does not look like a restaurant.'
'I must admit when we first came we were a little confused. It seems as though you are entering someone's house.'

'Yes, Madame.'
'I always liked that,' he said.
'Yes, sir.'
'And you are going to change?'
'Perhaps, sir. Everything must change with time.'
'Talking of time,' she said. 'It's getting late.'
'Yes,' he said. 'We must be going. Can we book to come again?'
'Of course, sir.'
He left and returned with the book.
'When would you like?'
He looked at his wife. She smiled with that smile that he loved so much.
'You choose,' she said.
'Shall we book for another three?'
'That's fine, love.'
He entered the dates into the book and the waitress returned with the bill.
'How long are you staying for this year?' the owner asked.
'Oh, the usual time.'
'And what are your plans?'
'Nothing really. Just sit and read by the pool. Take each day as it comes. Relax.'
'Can I recommend a place for you to go? It is a beautiful place, sir. Magnificent views. Away from all the tourists.'
'It sounds interesting,' she said.
'It is a small village on the west coast. You can park your car, take a picnic and walk a little way onto the headland and sit. The views are spectacular. You have the sea and the cliffs. Whenever I go there, it lifts my spirit.'

'Is there a beach?'
'Yes, Madame. You could go down to the beach if wanted to.'
'Is it far?' he asked.
'It is about fifty kilometres. You drive to the end of the motorway and head for Aljezur. It is past Aljezur. Keep going and it will be signposted. It is a beautiful drive, sir. You will enjoy it.'
'Good.'
'It is called Zambujeira do Mar, sir. I will write it down for you.'
He took a pen from his pocket and wrote the name on a piece of paper. They got up from the table.
'Thank you for a lovely evening,' she said. 'The food was wonderful as usual.'
'Thank you, Madame.'
'Yes, thank you,' he said and held out his hand.
'You are most welcome, sir,' he said, as they shook hands. 'Please find time to go to Zambujeira.'
He smiled and said, 'We will go tomorrow.'

It was late morning when they set off. They raced along the motorway, sealed in their air-conditioned car. At the end of the motorway they took the road over the hills and soon they were caught in a tail of traffic following an old lorry. He could see no reason to try to overtake and rush on ahead. They had the rest of the day ahead of them. He slowed down and was content to let others pass. He switched off the air-conditioning and wound down the windows. The car was filled by the smell of eucalyptus. They followed the road, marked yellow on the map, through Aljezur and Odeceixe. The road to Zambujeira was marked as no more than a track on the map. It led through sparse woodland and sun baked fields. As they reached the headland, the track opened out onto a bare piece of land used as a car park. He pulled into a space and closed the windows.

'This doesn't look much, does it?' he grumbled.

A deserted church and broken house seemed to lean against each other, as though exhausted by the passing of days in the constant heat.

'Let's get out and see,' she said, unclipping her seat belt and opening the door.

He reached for his hat to protect himself from the sun and realised he had left it behind. He struggled out of the car and stretched to ease the pain in his back and release the cramp from his foot.

'Let's follow this path,' she said. 'It looks as though it's the way we should go.'

As he pressed the button on the key, the car's lock clunked into place. He could feel the sun burning the top of his head and knew that he would suffer.

'I've forgotten my hat.'

'You'll be alright.'

He held her hand.

'Come on then. Silly to come all this way for nothing.'

They passed the church and he noticed a for sale sign nailed to the side of the house. She saw him looking at the sign.

'Don't get any ideas,' she laughed. 'You know we couldn't afford it.'

'We could just take a look.'

He walked over to a window and peered inside. Rubble was scattered across the floor. A crude stairway clung to the far wall. Fragments of furniture were piled in a corner. A water pipe had been twisted from the wall and dripped its brown stain onto the stone floor. A thick rope hung from an exposed joist. A faint smell of urine seeped out through the broken glass.

'No,' he said. 'It would be too much for me to repair.'

'Let's find this view,' she said, holding out her hand to him. 'That's what we came for. Remember?'

They followed the path and soon, ahead of them, they saw a bench, a place to rest.

As they approached, he could hear the sea. And then, suddenly, it was there before them! The waves of the great ocean pounding against the huge granite cliffs that stretched away in the distance. They stood in awe, transfixed by the sight and sound of such power and beauty. Unable to speak, they sat on the bench and gazed in wonder. Each time the ocean slammed against the land, the ground and air shook. He closed his eyes. There was no shade from the burning sun.

Death was coming. He knew it. He had felt its presence throughout his life, like the waves beneath. Grandparents, parents and friends; each caught by the great wave and swept away. And now he knew it would be him. The disease, which had taken his father, was crouching in his lungs, waiting. The irritating cough that had broken his sleep was the sign. His father's death had pushed him into going to the doctor, who had confirmed his fear. He had never smoked, but a childhood spent in rooms filled with blue clouds had been the cause. An innocent child poisoned by his parents' addiction. He had laughed, when the doctor told him. All his working life, his parents had been worried that he might be killed by a thug with a knife or a gun. Each night they would pray that God would protect him. His mother would whisper her blessed psalm 121 whenever they visited him. She would touch his hand and smile, assured that God would preserve him from all evil. Her faith, she would say, gave her the comfort of God's peace. And it had been her greatest wish that, one day, he would also find that faith. But he never had, because he had seen too much suffering and evil in the world. Not just in his work. Man's inhumanity seemed to spread throughout time.

Oh, he knew about God's being there in the acts of kindness and His sharing in the suffering. He knew that God did not want us to accept suffering as His will but that he wanted us to do something about it, not just blame God. He knew that! And he knew that life was full of suffering and that suffering could be seen as a problem or even a gift that could help him become better, wiser. And he knew there were limits between what he understood and what God wanted. And he knew that we were all born innocent and became responsible beings, who had to deal with that responsibility and do our best with what we knew and could do. And he knew that, at the end of this world of suffering, God had more to give and that there was the hope of healing in His time, when we would have a joyful communion with God and that all the suffering would be worth it. All we had to do was trust in God's love and no person would be wasted. All would be healed, saved. He knew that. He had heard it from the Christian, from the Jew, from the Muslim, from the Hindu and from the Buddhist. But he could not believe it. Oh, there was an order to things, but it was not a divine order. It was not due to God or to fate. It was an order that was indifferent to mankind's struggle to survive, to understand. And life and death were just part of that order.

Sometimes he wished he could believe, have that blind faith in the perversity of God's work in our sacred lives. But he couldn't.

Suddenly she touched his hand.

'Are you alright?'

'Yes, love. It's just the sun. I should have brought my hat.'

'I've been thinking,' she said. 'I want to die first…'

'What?'

'It has to be me, who dies first…I don't want to be left without you.'

'Don't be daft. I'm not going to leave you.'

'I know, but I don't want you to die before me.'

'Well, I'll see what I can do.'

'I'm serious! I don't know what I'd do without you.'

'Come here, you daft thing,' he said and put his arm around her.

The waves crashed against the cliffs below.

They sat for a long time and, eventually, she said, 'Come on; let's go, before you get one of your headaches.'

They got up from the bench and walked past the broken church and house. He knew he would never return. This would be their last journey together.

When they got back to the car, someone had left a bunch of flowers on the bonnet and a dog had pissed against the wheels.

The ending…

"May the angels
lead you into paradise."

In paradisum.

During the debate on the Abortion Bill, a Muslim and Christian agreed on the concept of 'ensoulment'. The Christian believed that the soul entered the body at the moment of conception, the Muslim forty to one hundred and twenty days later.

Do other animals have souls?

1.

Herod had killed three times before.

When he was a child, in the midst of summer, flying ants emerged from the earth, drawn out by the heat of the sun, and covered the kitchen windows in a dark crawling mass. His mother screamed and his father cursed, as the ants found a way into the house. His father closed the windows and the door, while his mother poured water into the kettles and placed them on top of the old stove. They waited for the water to boil and watched the ants gather in their silence.
'This must be like the plagues in the bible,' his mother whispered.
'The plague would have been worse than this,' his father laughed. 'That was locusts!'
'Imagine!' his mother gasped.
The kettles sputtered and wheezed and began their siren scream. His father wrapped the handles in rags and lifted them from the stove.
'Open the door!' he called.
'Don't let them in!' his mother warned.
As his father carried the kettles, gurgling with their fierce water, he opened the door.
'Come on then, son. Close the door behind you!'
The air seemed to be filled with ants. They swarmed about them, crashing into their faces, their mouths, clinging to their hair and ears.
'Here you are!'
His father handed him a kettle.
'Be careful! Look for their entrance! I'll do the windows first.'

He could feel the weight of the water as it moved in the kettle. The rag was hot in his hand. His father began to trickle the boiled water carefully over the ants, washing them from the window. He searched the ground for the entrance to the nest. His shoes were already covered in ants. He stamped his feet and kicked against a large stone. Water slopped from the spout of the kettle and fell onto his shoe. He brushed an ant from the side of his mouth and waved them away from his eyes.

'Pour in as much as you can!' his father shouted.

Ants were on his sleeves, his hands. They were crawling in his hair and ears.

'There it is, look!'

His father was pointing to a crack in the ground. It looked like the soil beneath was coming to life, as though the Earth was purging itself. He carried the kettle to the tangled mass and poured out its scalding heat. A thick bloom erupted from the hole and a dark stain spread its stillness across the ground. He poured and watched as the ants became a black scum and their lace wings floated across the concrete into the grass. Ants, about to spread their wings to take flight, were carried away in the flood.

His father joined him.

'Well done!' he said. 'Let's get some more water.'

He emptied the dregs from the kettle. The air seemed to be clearing.

'Just get these off you,' his father sighed, brushing the ants from him. 'Your mother wouldn't want them in the house.'

It was then he felt the pain in his foot. The hot water had seeped through and found his skin. He grimaced.

'What's wrong?'
'Some water got into my shoe.'
'Let's get you inside.'
His father carried the kettles and opened the kitchen door.
'Don't let them in!' his mother called. 'I don't want them…'
She saw the pain on his face.
'What's the matter?'
'Some water got in his shoe.'
'Get it off…Let's have a look.'
He sat in a chair and his father removed his shoe. The top of his sock was wet.
'Here, let me,' said his mother, bringing a cold, wet cloth. 'You get the burn cream. It's in the cupboard.'
His mother knelt before him and gently placed his foot in her lap.
'How did it happen?'
'It just spilled from the kettle.'
'Let's see…'
She rolled down the sock to his ankle and lifted it over the top of his foot. The skin was marked scald-red.
'This may hurt a little…'
She placed the cloth onto his wound and pressed softly. The cold water trickled down in between his toes. He winced.
'It'll be all right,' she whispered. 'It'll be all right.'
His father brought the cream.
'Do we need to take him to the hospital?' he asked.
'No…I think he'll be fine.'
'Will it blister?'
'Probably…'
She removed the cloth and dried his foot.

'There you are…Not so bad.'
He could feel the skin tightening.
'Let's just put a bit of this on…'
The cream felt ice-cold against the burn and made him flinch.
'It hurts!'
'I know, my love…But this will help take the pain away and help it to heal…'
He watched his mother's delicate fingers spreading the cream over the burn and listened to her soothing voice.
'You'll be all right,' she said. 'You'll be all right.'
And he knew it was true.
Later that day, when his father had destroyed all the ants and his mother had bandaged his wounded foot, he asked them whether the ants had felt the pain like him. No, they assured him. Ants were not like him. They did not feel things like him. They were just ants. For a moment he was uncertain. But then he remembered their silence and knew that what his parents had said must be true.

One year, at the beginning of spring, when the ground was wet and the soil still cold, his father asked him to help in the garden. By the shed was a mound of soil covered in dead leaves and surrounded by rotting branches. It needed to be cleared so that his father could repair a broken fence. The branches could be taken in the barrow and piled up in the corner of the garden. The leaves could be taken and emptied into a bin to make compost and the soil could be spread across the ground.
He began by loading the branches into the barrow. Some were dry and broke easily beneath his feet.

Some were large and sodden with the weight of a winter's aging. They crumbled in his hands as he raised them from their bed of leaves. Lice, tipped onto their backs by this sudden upheaval, arched themselves to gain a foothold, and crawled instinctively back to their damp darkness. The branches hit the side of the barrow with a soft clump. He worked steadily, testing the weight of each barrow load before wheeling it across the garden to the opposite corner. As he tipped them out, he was reminded of a programme he had seen, where the bodies of people called Jews were poured into a pit. His father had said that he could watch it, that he needed to know that it had happened.

It did not take long to clear the branches. It did not take long to fill the pit.

He took the rake and began to gather up the wet leaves. It was easy enough. A gentle rhythm. Throw the head of the rake out and pull it in. Throw it out and pull it in. Make a small heap and pile the cold mass into the barrow.

He threw out the head of the rake and felt the old, smooth handle flow through his hands and the steel-hard prongs thump into the mound.

A shriek burst from the leaves. The rake twitched in his hand, a dull pulse. He dropped the handle and stared at the head of the rake. Nothing moved. He waited. A cloud's chilled shadow touched his shoulder and the mound darkened. He rubbed his hands against his jeans and gently kicked against the handle. The head of the rake rose from the dead leaves, turned on its side and fell onto its back as though exhausted. Wet, pierced leaves clung to the rake's teeth. A frog pressed against the earth, trying to find the damp darkness that had been its safe place, and lurched to one side. It pressed again. One leg pushed hard, making the frog roll down the side of the mound onto its back, exposing its pale belly and pulsing throat. It kicked its one leg and squirmed on its back, a frantic motion to right itself.

He bent down and tried to pick it up. The frog kicked and kicked against his palms, writhing within his delicate grasp. The shock of such a fearful life force made him release it. The frog leapt from his hands and hung in the air. He tried to catch it and juggled its small, slimy mass until it finally tumbled free and thumped into the ground. Its left leg was stretched out from its body.

He ran to fetch his father.

'Come quickly,' he shouted. 'There's a frog. There's something wrong with it.'

His father left his work and followed him.

'All right, son. It's only a frog.'

'But there's something wrong with it!'

'Let's have a look.'

He led his father back to the dark corner. It was beginning to rain.

'Look…There'

He pointed to the frog's folded form with its stretched out leg.

'What's wrong with it?'

His father picked a small cane, crouched down and touched the leg. The frog twitched. Its throat pulsed. Its eyes stared their endless stare.

'Is it hurt?'

Gleet oozed from the wound in its side.

'Yes, I'm afraid so…Look.'

He used the cane to expose the wound.
'Is it dead?'
'No, not yet…'
'I didn't mean to do it! I didn't know it was there! I tried to pick it up and help it but I couldn't hold it. It…'
'It's all right. It's not your fault. Just an accident…'
'What can we do?'
His father gave a deep sigh and looked at the frog.
'You go in and wash your hands in hot soapy water.'
He looked at his palms and saw the marks.
'I didn't mean to…'
'I know. It's all right. Go in and wash your hands…I'll sort it out.'
'What will you do?'
'It'll be all right…Go and wash your hands.'
He looked at the frog.
'Is it going to be all right?'
His father stood up.
'Come on, let's get you inside…'
He placed his hands gently on his son's shoulders and led him down the path in the rain. When they reached the back door his father said, 'Go inside. I need to put the spade away so it doesn't get wet.'
'What about the frog?'
'Don't worry about it…Go on, quick, before you get soaked.'
His father opened the door.
'Call your mother,' he said. 'And try not to touch anything.'
He went inside and scuffed off his boots. His father closed the door. He called to his mother and explained. She took him to the sink in the kitchen and ran

some hot water into a bowl. As he washed his hands, he watched his father collect the spade, carry it into the dark space by the shed and raise it above his head.

Later that day, when the rain had stopped, he returned to the mound. The frog had gone. In a quiet place flies were feeding on its eyes.

They walked out into the wilderness together, the boy and his dog. Through the half-deserted streets, across the roads, out of the town, the dog strained at the leash, gasping for air.

Reaching the open ground, the boy released the chain from the dog's neck. Freed from the restraints of house, garden, town, they raced through the long grass together.

When the boy grew tired, the dog bounded into the bushes, disappeared for a while and then reappeared to come charging towards him. The boy laughed as the dog leaped around him, 'Come with me! Come with me! Come and play! We are free! Free!'

The boy walked on, crossed the fields and climbed the hill with the dog running off to sniff the ground, always returning to his side. When they reached the top they sat together, backs turned to the town, to gaze in silence at the moors below and the distant hills.

At their back, from time to time, they heard the sound of horns and motors in the town, brought to them on the wind, which blew through them and passed across the moor to lose itself in the wilderness. They leant against each other, safe in their own company and content with the joy of being. The boy felt the panting weight of the dog against him. They sat for a long time, the sun beating down on them, their souls stretched tight across the sky.

On their way back, the dog found a stick, brought it to the boy and dropped it at his feet. The boy picked it up and the dog sat, his body filled with excitement. The boy smiled.

'Go on then,' he said and threw.

The dog raced after the stick, grasped it between his jaws, charged back to the boy and dropped it at his feet again. It sat, tail wagging, body twitching, jaws gaping, tongue lolling, eyes filled with excitement. He threw it again. The dog turned and bounded after the stick, which cartwheeled through the air. It hit the ground and bounced up. The dog jumped, caught it and ran back. It dropped the stick at his feet and looked up at him.

'Again. Throw it again.'

He picked it up and felt the wet slime. He made to throw the stick again and the dog raced away. It gathered speed across the ground and tumbled to a halt, when it realised the stick had not appeared. It turned, confused and saw the stick in the boy's hand. The boy laughed and threw the stick away. The dog rushed back and hurtled past the boy. The stick lay in the grass. The dog dragged it out, carried it back to the boy and dropped it at his feet.

They played for a long time. When the boy had had enough, the dog leapt around him caught in the frenzy of excitement. The boy dropped the stick, only for the dog to pick it up and drop it at his feet again, barking, urging him to play on.

'No, no more,' the boy said and walked away. The dog picked up the stick and followed him. They walked across the ground, cracked by the sun. When they reached the field's boundary, the dog dropped the stick. The boy opened the gate. The dog passed through and the boy placed the choke chain around the dog's neck.

As they followed the road back to the town, the dog was no longer pulling. They trudged along the pavements, keeping to the shadows of hedges and walls. The boy could feel his head pounding and knew that a migraine was gathering. Small shapes began to float across his vision. The dog walked slowly behind him, struggling to keep up. Suddenly, in a street of scattered bricks, the dog stopped.

'Come on,' the boy said, as the pain began to grip the back of his eye. He pulled gently at the leash. The dog lowered its head, heaved and retched up a pool of thick, putrid slime. It began to shake.

'Come on, boy,' the boy encouraged, a wave of panic surging through the pain. 'Come on…Not far…Nearly home.'

The dog's eyes were the colour of congealed blood. The remnants of the slime hung from its jaw.

'Come on…You can do it.'

The dog began to walk slowly, unable to raise its head.

'That's it…Good boy…Nearly there.'

They walked slowly together, each of them in their own pain.

When they reached the gate, the dog collapsed. The boy's father rushed out to them.

'Where have you been?' he shouted. 'Your mother's been worried sick. Do you know what time it is? What's happened?'

'We were playing…'

His father noticed the pain in his face.

'Are you all right?' he asked, anger turning to concern.
'Migraine.'
'Get yourself inside. I'll bring him in.'
His father knelt beside the dog.
'He's been sick,' the boy explained.
'I can see,' his father said as he raised the dog's body from the ground. 'Go on. Get in. Get some pills and get to bed. I'll sort this out.'
They went round to the back of the house and into the kitchen.
'What on earth?' gasped his mother, pushing back her chair.
'The dog's been sick and collapsed,' his father said. 'And he needs some pills. He's got one of his migraines. Both been out in the sun too long.'
His mother got the pills from the cupboard and filled a glass with water, while his father laid the dog on the floor, got a rag from under the kitchen sink and soaked it in water. The boy took the pills and drank the cold water as he watched his father wipe the dog's jaws.
'I'm sorry, dad.'
'You get upstairs to bed.'
'Will he be all right?'
'I don't know. We'll sort it out. You get to bed.'
He climbed the stairs, got undressed, closed the curtains and got into bed. The intense pain and the worry about his dog swirled together. He pressed his head into the pillow, lay in the dark and prayed that it would all pass in the night. But he could not lie still. He tossed and turned, knowing that if the dog died, it would be his fault. He was to blame.
In the night, when he had settled, he dreamed of standing by the dog's grave.

His father: 'He was in pain, my son. He suffers no more.'
His mother: 'He is at peace now, waiting for you in heaven.'

And in the morning, when he woke, the dog was there, sitting at the end of his bed.
'Good,' he said. 'You are awake at last. Come and play.'

2
Winter.
They happened upon some old photographs
Jumbled together in an old box
This is me with my father, when I was three
This is me in the garden, when I was five
This is me leaving, when I was eighteen
This is me with you, when I was twenty
This is us, married, when we were twenty four
This is us, when were thirty
This is us, when we were forty
This is us, when we were fifty...
They smiled at each other as they sorted through and placed them in order back into the box.
And then he found the old school photograph
And there he was, seated in the second row
And behind him stood Herod, like a shadow.
As he went to bed that night, he caught sight of himself in the mirror.
For a moment
He could not recognise the face
Nor remember the name.

3

On a cold night, which warned of a hard morning frost, he turned a corner and saw Orion, stretched out across a clear, dark sky. He had not seen it for some time and was shocked by its sudden presence. He stopped and gazed in awe. Although he knew he was looking at a great illusion, he could not shake off the sense that what was before him had been there in the time of his ancestors and would endure forever. And, for a moment, for a brief precious moment, he felt that he was part of it all, that he would also endure forever. As Orion stood before him, in its vast indifference, he smiled, shook off the deception, as though awakening from a dream, and walked home to his beloved wife...

He scattered the ashes in the safe place

Beneath the Acer tree

And there, among the fallen leaves,

Were their names

For everyone to see.

From the son

At last I have found a home and, like God, can be born of Man, become a living being.
I lie here in my secret life, listening to her heart, as it moves our shared blood, and I dream such dreams!
And, beyond this safe place, my name and the dark future waits for me…

Epicurus:

Is God willing to prevent evil, but not able? Then he is impotent. Is he able, but not willing? Then he is malevolent. Is he both able and willing? Whence then is evil?

Chuang-Tzu:

I dreamt I was a butterfly, flitting around and enjoying myself. I had no idea I was Chuang-Tzu. Then, suddenly, I woke up and was Chuang-Tzu again. But I could not tell, had I been Chuang-Tzu dreaming I was a butterfly, or a butterfly dreaming I was Chuang-Tzu.

If you want to comment on this book
email the author John Squires at
herod_dreams@live.co.uk

Further copies of the book can be ordered from
Mathom House Publishing via:

Email johnpearce@ntlworld.com

Mathom House Publishing
152 Carter Lane East
South Normanton
**Derbyshire
DE55 2DZ**